The Ardent Artist Books

# *Broken*

# OBSESSION

## *Part Two*

# *Trisha Fuentes*

BROKEN OBSESSION – PART TWO
WRITTEN BY TRISHA FUENTES

This book is a work of fiction. All names, characters and places are used fictitiously. Historical figures, celebrity names, trademarks, songs, brand names, street names and likenesses are the sole property and copyright of their respective authors. All written material is copyright of Trisha Fuentes. Cover image by BigStockPhoto. Reuse and/or reproduction of any written material are strictly prohibited.

This book may not be reproduced, transmitted, or stored in whole or in part by any means, including graphic, electronic, or mechanical without the express written consent of the publisher.

Copyright © 2009 Trisha Fuentes
ISBN: 978-0-9825797-0-1

For Zach...

Hoping he will choose Plan A
Instead of Plan B

# CHAPTER ONE

*Las Vegas, Nevada*

Reverend Michael Mulroney had seen couples come and go.  Having been the **Wedding's in Heaven** minister for nearly twenty years, he's had his fair share of outlandish, fabulous, imaginary, both dazzling and humbled a wedded pair.  He's seen celebrities grope and tear at their clothes while saying their vows only to hear that they had the union annulled two days later.  He's officiated over pairs as old as ninety and as young as sixteen; pregnant, obese, mixed race, dwarfs, drunk, sober, foreign couples, once even a mob boss (who happened to be the father of the bride) that held a shot gun to his soon to be son-in-law's terrified head at the altar.  But that union was hush-hush and Reverend Mulroney was sworn to secrecy over that little wedding; and last he heard, the man was elected recently into state government and the couple had four grown children and were **still** married.

But without a doubt, his favorite to pledge in marriage was a couple who seemed truly in love, a man and woman who he knew in his heart were destined to be married and stay coupled **forever**.

Stationed before him was one of those pairs, the chap couldn't take his eyes off his ladylove.  They held each other's hands intimately and only a few feet apart and not once had they glared around them or at other guests. They acted as if they were the only two people in the room; in love and on the cusp of rapture, and that's how it should be, Reverend Mulroney decided.

"Do you Eduardo; take Amber as your lawfully wedded wife?" Reverend Mulroney asked the tall man, who wasn't about to tear his eyes away from his lovely raven-haired lady.

"I would...forever, I would."

"And do you Amber, take Eduardo—"

"Yes, I would."

The Reverend cleared his throat, "I haven't finished yet."

Amber gazed over at the Reverend's eyes, her hazel eyes widened with emotion, "I'm sorry...but I would."

The Reverend smiled, the love he could distinguish in her eyes alone warmed his very toes. "By the power invested in me, I now pronounce you husband and—"

The Reverend rolled his eyes once again because the couple didn't even allow him to finish his pronouncement! The lofty man grabbed the woman's head from behind and brought her mouth up to his. Their kiss, so sensual and impassioned, brought on a few gasps of surprise by even his witnesses! They braced their bodies with such force; they practically glued themselves together.

"...Wife," he finished, "You may kiss the bride." The Reverend looked away from the couple and over at the two smiling and crying women that had been the couple's witnesses; the older woman was holding a little boy—a fidgety little boy, the Reverend thought, who looked remarkably similar to the bride.

"Congratulations!" Sheila Thomas, Amber's mother exclaimed, throwing her arms up in the air and reaching out for her daughter to give her a fond hug.

Amber towered over her petite mother and leaned down to give her a meaningful hug. "Oh I love you mom, I'm so happy right now."

"Oh I know darling, I can imagine," Sheila said in return, closing her eyes and feeling her daughters radiating joy.

"Your big sis needs a hug too!" Molly Fitzgerald, Amber's older sister exclaimed, reaching out to give Amber another fond squeeze. "I'm so happy for you Amber!"

"Oh Eduardo, the ceremony was short but absolutely beautiful, I don't think I've ever cried so much at a wedding before, especially at any of my six," Sheila joked, hugging her son-in-law near. He too, had to bend down to give Sheila a hug.

Eduardo reached into his pant pockets and pulled out two key cards. "Sheila—Molly, there are two suites at the Bellagio waiting for you, meet us tomorrow in the lobby at five, we have a seven o'clock flight to catch."

Sheila looked at her son-in-law bewildered. "What," she asked in dismay, looking down at the key cards with the Bellagio emblem engraved on their front.

"Where are you going? I thought we were going to a reception!" Molly teased, watching her sister and brother-in-law wrap their arms about one another in unison and walk toward the chapel exit.

Eduardo gave his sister-in-law a far too burning grin. "Everything's paid for in the suite, room service, and massages, day care if you want to go down to the casino and gamble a little bit. You even have a couple thousand free of charge to spend on whatever entertainment you desire. Thanks for being here, I don't know where I'd be without you Sheila-Molly, I love you both, but now I have to be alone with my wife."

Amber gazed up at her husband and caressed his cheek with her hand. She then gave a friendly good-bye and blew a kiss to her son.

Sheila rolled her eyes. "Looks like the honeymoon has already started," she replied, watching Eduardo practically ravish Amber's neck passionately.

Does happily ever after really exist? It does for Amber and Eduardo Sanchez.

It's true and incredulous to believe that Eduardo Sanchez was once Amber's brother-in-law. But if she had met him first, she would have married him in a heartbeat. The two of them were meant to be; soul mates, one half the same person. They had been to hell and back and never believed that they'd really be together after all the lying and deceiving that they did. Fifteen years of loving each other secretly and continuing a three-year physical affair, until one-day Amber decided she wanted more from their clandestine relations and asked Eduardo to leave his wife, her sister-in-law, Leticia, for her. Eduardo balked at the idea, claiming the scandal would destroy his family and opted to continue on with their affair. Amber was willing to do anything for Eduardo and decided she was going to leave her husband and her kids for him, why wouldn't he do the same? Eduardo had misrepresented himself all those years and they never really did have any kind of future. Telling her that he loved her was just a device to continue on with their affair. She felt like a fool back then because she kept on falling for his unvarying charm and Amber felt used, discarded, ashamed and unwanted. Her Father Figure didn't want her anymore and Eduardo forced Amber into making a harrowing obsessive irreversible decision, causing Amber to try to take her own life.

The moment they arrived on their floor, Eduardo scooped up his bride and walked her down to the honeymoon suite on top of the Bellagio hotel. They were kissing and necking the whole way through and Eduardo nearly buckled under his knees when he reached the doorway. "The key card," he breathed, not venturing far from Amber's heavenly skin.

"Where?" She quietly mouthed, roaming his pant pockets searching for the card. Amber beamed when she found something else inside his pants. Solid and tempting, Eduardo's erection was tough to ignore.

Amber sliced the key card across the electronic door lock and the door immediately opened. Eduardo then nudged the door open wider with his knee and dropped Amber's thighs so she could maintain her balance immediately.

"Over the threshold, now onto consummating this union," he breathed, grabbing his wife into his arms and immobilizing Amber against the suite wall. He wanted to devour her—he waited so Goddamn long. Sixteen months since they last made love. Sixteen months since he last kissed her like this. Hot burning passion consumed him as he continued to buss her skin, up and down her neck, her shoulders, hurriedly ripping off all her garments.

Amber opened up her eyes and surveyed the suite. The room was exquisite...**oh God that was nice**...the space was stunning! The bed, the couch, the view...**oh good Lord, Eduardo was naughty!** Amber looked down at him as he knelt to the ground and released Amber of her white slacks then her underwear.

"Good God Amber," Eduardo huskily uttered, "I want to practically eat you—you taste so good." Eduardo allowed his hands to roam her body at will, all the while kissing her flat stomach, tonguing her navel, up her mid section then circling around her nipples. "Excuse me," he roughly expressed, "I apologize for not being patient," he breathed through sucking her bust, "but I've waited so long—I'm a little out of control."

Amber smiled and watched her husband as he practically engulfed every inch of her upper body; trying to fit her plump mounds into his entire mouth, continuing to grind her erotically and spiraling a runway inferno between her legs. She instantly brought to mind the first time they had made love. Eduardo had her up against the hotel room wall, like he was doing now; his body compressed against hers in a seductive animalistic way. She couldn't even move, his leg was between hers and she nearly climaxed from the way he pressed against her carnally, granulating and bringing her to a mania she needed controlled. He was doing that now and he was such a vulgar psychopath! "You are such a tease! Enough already with the foreplay! Would you just fuck me already?" Amber pleaded, feeling Eduardo's mouth release from her body and brought up to hers awarding her a wicked grin before lifting her up and throwing her to the bed.

Amber's known him for more than fifteen years, but had only been sleeping with him for the past three. She married his younger brother Victor right out of high school, but knew something was missing in their marriage from the very beginning.

Passion.

Amber always craved the love she missed by not having a stable Father Figure in her life, one daddy and the strength of an authority in her life; and late in her marriage she realized the reason why she was so attracted to Eduardo in the first place, he produced that fervor she never had with her husband.  She had love in abundance though, from Victor loving her, worshipping her, but Amber always felt incomplete, as if she was walking around with an outer shell surrounding her body.  When Victor would kiss her, when they would make love, there was always something absent from their intimacy.

The day she met Eduardo, he was twenty-five and just home from graduating Harvard Law School, and boy, was he something else.  Arrogant as hell and so lovely to look at, he was single then and owned his sexuality.  Amber never met anyone so incredibly confident before!  They were friends first and Eduardo held back his infatuation for Amber while Amber and his brother got married, had a child, bought a house and made another baby.  He fell in love with Amber on their first meeting, but restrained himself in fear of losing his brother's trust.

Eduardo at forty was like fine wine and just as sexy.  Having matured well, Eduardo was still employed by the high-priced Century City law firm, Aldridge & Watson.  He was well known in the legal community and considered somewhat a celebrity defense attorney now and oftentimes had his picture taken by the paparazzi alongside his movie star clientele, and, at six feet four inches tall, Eduardo Sanchez was not only intimidating in height, but exuded confidence and charm.  And, as of late, Eduardo couldn't walk into a room without every head turning to gape at him.  Men included, Eduardo was a man to be envied.  He was accustomed to grabbing the attention of crowds and exercised his magnetism skillfully.

And with women...well, let's just say with green eyes, nut-brown hair, broad shoulders, slim waist, lean hips and muscular chest, women all around him couldn't help but fall head over heels in love with Eduardo Sanchez, Esq. at first sight.

But with all the attentiveness he's endured over the years, with considerate focus from females alone, there was still just one woman he's ever truly loved.  One solitary female that stirred the nerves in his stomach when he looked at her, one particular woman he allowed to ruin his trust with his family, break a bond with his brother and one woman who he'd walk through fire for...**did** walk through fire for, and that was his wife.

Amber Fitzgerald Sanchez...now his wife, for the rest of her life!

Eduardo made sure that his wife got everything she ever dreamed of when she woke up from her comatose state.  Before her despondency, Amber stated that she wanted to wake up in each other's arms, take walks on the beach and go away together.  After their brief stay in Las Vegas they were off to the islands of Fiji—where Eduardo had arranged a four-week stay on a very secluded island.

# CHAPTER TWO

Turtle Island to be exact and Eduardo had rented the entire island for the month. Turtle Island provided an all-exclusive exotic vacation with private beaches and breathtaking crystal blue water. The site of the film location "Blue Lagoon" starring Brooke Shields, Turtle Island was the closest thing to heaven on Earth for the newlywed couple.

Amber and Eduardo were at the resort, checking in their baggage, when Eduardo grabbed Amber by her waist and brought her body into his for a kiss. Amber wrapped her arms around his neck and melted into happiness.

The attendant handed the twosome their keys and was chagrined at the sight of the couple groping each other's bodies as if they were alone.

Eduardo broke apart from Amber and held out his hand for the man to place the key in. "Bring our bags to us in about two hours—"

"Four," Amber corrected him, smiling and not venturing off from his erotic gaze.

"Six," Eduardo grinned back at her, shoving the keys into his pants pocket.

"Six!" Amber hooted. "Oh my, planning for an adventure, Mr. Sanchez?"

Eduardo grabbed her into him again as Amber flung her head back feeling Eduardo twirl her body around into a circular motion.

The moment they reached their private bungalow, their clothes escaped their bodies. Amber pulled his shirt over his head, Eduardo unzipped her skirt and Amber drew down his pants while Eduardo unhooked her bra, and there they stayed, naked and alone with another for nearly four days.

Amber came out of the bathroom dressed in a Hawaiian motif sarong and turquoise bikini top intending on visiting the beach. Eduardo's mouth dropped open wide, she looked absolutely gorgeous. Her hourglass figure tight and lean; her breasts sprung to attention and he couldn't keep his eyes off her 34-D's.

Amber beamed and posed for him in the doorway. "I see that you like it?"

"Are you kidding? We're not going to make it to the beach dear girl."

Amber whined, "Oh, you promised! I want to see the ocean at least once while I'm here. We've done nothing but make love for four days!"

"And my wife is complaining?" Eduardo guffawed, "Most wives would be jealous of you and your insatiable husband."

Amber thought about it, smiled and then headed for the door, taunting him. Eduardo grabbed her waist from behind and pulled her body back in. "Oh no, you're not getting away dressed like that."

"Eduardo, you are so bad!" Amber teased at him, grabbing his neck and pulling him in for a soft hearted kiss.

"I know, now undress for me," he demanded, leaning back on the bed, enjoying the burlesque show. Good God, he loved to look at her! Long raven hair, draping over the sides of her silky shoulders, her soft supple complexion mixed over her honey-toned skin. Her eyes, Good God, how he loved her eyes! Hazel, mesmerizing, shades of brown, blue and green. The attribute he loved most about Amber was her natural beauty. She never wore make up, her eyelashes were always dark, her lips and cheeks always covered in a pink hue, her face so trouble-free and lustrous—his wife was radiant day or night.

Amber started to blush and then slowly unraveled her sarong; underneath was a new turquoise-blue bathing bikini, but kept it on until she took her top off. Untying it slowly, she watched in delight as a sense of triumph arose when she noticed her husband's eyes transform from yellow-green to a deep dark emerald. She eyed his body up and down as his legs grew wide and his erection rose to the opportunity. Amber then slowly peeled down her bikini top to expose her luscious generous breasts and tackled him rolling their bodies romantically over the bed.

That night on the beach, the twosome finally made it out of the bungalow and lay down side by side on lounge chairs, dipping their toes in the crystal blue water watching the sun about to set.

"Tell me about Peyton," Amber asked softly, reaching over to caress a few strands of Eduardo's hair that mussed up his gorgeous face.

Peyton Enrique Sanchez, age two, was an extension of their love and the miracle that brought their involvement full circle. He was born to Amber and Eduardo while Amber was still unconscious. It had been a miracle that she was even expectant at all for Amber suffered from endometriosis and was scheduled to have a hysterectomy when she and Eduardo had their traumatic fight causing her to lie in a coma for sixteen months.

"Tell me about my son."

"What do you want to know?"

"Has it been hard? Raising him, without me?"

"Your mother has been very helpful."

"Really? My mother?" Amber said astonished, disbelieving the facts as he relayed them to her. Her last heart-to-heart conversation with her mother ended with Sheila being displeased about their affair and that she thought Eduardo had been using her to suit his ego.

"Let me tell you something about your mother," Eduardo voiced, stroking his wife's fingers over and over. "Your mother is a Godsend. She amazes me with how much life she's lived and how much she knows and what a big heart she has. I love your mother and our son does too."

"Really? How so?"

"Peyton lights up like a firefly when he's around her," he gushed, holding Amber's hand tight. "She plays with him, and he responds to her gentleness; she really is a great-grandmother," he let go, thinking of his own mother and father at that moment.

"And your mom, have you spoken to them yet?"

Eduardo closed his mouth and then gazed out toward the ocean. "No," he thought sadly, "They haven't forgiven me yet," he paused, swallowing some spit of shame, "It's going to take some time. Our family values are unwavering and deep."

Amber was insulted and laughed, "Oh yeah? Just because my mother has been married quite a few times, that automatically makes our values lesser than yours?"

Eduardo thought about it for a moment and then laughed along with her, "No, I didn't mean it that way, what I meant was that my mother and father are not as liberal as your mother is and not as forgiving. It will take some healing, but I think she'll soften with time. She's gonna wake up one morning and realize she's missed out on knowing another grandchild and she'll be curious."

"Do you think she'll really want to see him?"

"Yah, she loves all her nieces and nephews and I'm sure my Aunt's are all bothering her with their curiosity and gossip and it will definitely spark some kind of interest."

"And you? My husband, my love? Finally a full-time parent; unselfish and considerate?"

Eduardo smirked. "Our son," he surged, reaching over to Amber and moving her hair away from her shoulder, "Is amazing and surprises me every day. Sometimes late at night, when I'm unable to sleep, I go into Peyton's room and sit there and stare at him," he said, leaning over her and grabbing her hand away from his face to intertwine his fingers within hers. "I still can't believe he's ours."

"I still can't believe I was pregnant," Amber declared.

"Me either. I'll never forget watching him grow inside you. The doctor's all kept telling your mother and me that you would suffer a miscarriage, but you didn't. Peyton grew strong within your womb and now's he's just...precocious."

"Oh yah? How so?"

"Like I said, the boy is remarkable," he pronounced, lifting his jaw up to the sky. "He began talking at seven months and started to walk when he was nine; you've met him, he's so smart—he wants to be a doctor."

Amber started to laugh, "A doctor, already? How do you know?"

"Oh I know, he's always taking care of his stuffed animals, carrying around a little pad of paper and a pen, the boy is so focused. Mrs. Lopez is already speaking Spanish to him, and he's already conversing with her."

"Wonderful, you mean my son will be able to swear at me in Spanish while taking my temperature?"

Eduardo laughed, "Maybe even in French once I'm done with him."

Amber suddenly got up from the lounge chair and walked over to the waves and into the cobalt ocean. Eduardo followed her lead and grabbed her waist from behind; wrapping his arms around her midriff as she welcomed his embrace. They both look out at the vast clear blue sea beyond them and the beautiful array of orange daylight spread out across the horizon.

"I want to get to know him," Amber whispered out toward the water.

He grabbed her tight, "You will."

"I know that sounds awful, not knowing your own child."

Eduardo kissed Amber on her neck, "It was under special circumstances."

Amber closed her eyes from feeling special herself and twirled her body around within his confine, landing a deep kiss on his lips.

Eduardo accepted the enticement and grabbed her arm leading them back to lie down on one lounge chair this time.

Legs meshed through one another, Eduardo was on top of his wife, kissing her neck sensuously, when Amber heard her husband whisper into her ear, "Do you realize how happy I am?"

Feeling him tug at her underwear, she helped his hands draw them down to her ankles and away onto the sand before Amber dug her nails into his back. "Probably not had happy as I am," she breathed, meeting his erotic movement, so stimulating and so wonderfully flawless.

Eduardo's rigid flesh digs into her as Amber sucked him in buried beneath. "I don't think so," he exhaled, kissing his wife erotically, his tongue delving inside the depths of her mouth. He broke apart from her lips to pass his tongue behind her earlobe sending Amber into internal bliss. "I feel like this weight has been lifted off my shoulders," he murmured into her ear, plunging and cramming his wife full of his better part. "I'm about to combust," he wailed reaching his climax immediately.

Amber arched her back up as well and allowed her own pinnacle to burst and spread.

Eduardo continued to lie on her body, and Amber beamed. "God, I love you," she cried. "Do you realize how much I do?"

He kissed his wife with overzealous passion and moved inside her once more. "I know you do; I can feel it in the way you kiss me. Do you know how much I love you?"

Amber brought her torso up to him again and welcomed her husband's unappeasable enthusiasm. "I know you do; I can feel it in the way you make love to me."

Amber climaxed right away from Eduardo's expertise and felt her husband's body go limp and shiver once more when he reached another culmination. Amber opened up her eyes and stroked his back, "Eduardo? What's wrong?"

He didn't say anything, but continued to shed tears on the side of her neck. Amber felt his continual near-jerk reactions of him trying to stifle his emotions and Amber continued to embrace him and brought his body in further. She caressed his hair, his neck, and then finally pulled his shoulders up. Eduardo had tears in his eyes and she melted at the display. She kissed the salty wetness and wiped the dampness away with her fingers, "Baby...what's wrong?"

"I'm afraid," Eduardo eerily voiced, bowing his head back into her neck.

Amber pulled up her husband's head and made him look her in the face, "Afraid…afraid of what?"

He kissed her tenderly on the lips, "The repercussions," he remarked mysteriously, "The fallout of our actions."

At that very moment, a strange, unfamiliar pang darted through Amber's chest which made her apprehensive as well. He must have been contemplating this for quite some time to have kept it from her only allowing her to see his fear until now. Amber pulled her husband's body back down to hers. "Oh baby, I love you so much," she voiced running her fingers through his head of hair, "What you and I share, only a handful of people get to understand. Remember, we're soul mates, you and I; we're healthier together than we are apart and together we will overcome whatever tries to end us. Our love can conquer anything."

Eduardo started to snicker, "That's so cliché," he let go, starting to kiss Amber's neck once again. "Just know, that I will always love you Amber. I never want to experience those feelings I used to have when I wasn't with you. That obsession, it consumed me, I couldn't think, I couldn't even breathe when I saw you with my brother."

"We're not turning back baby, we're stepping forward and we're doing it together this time."

"I know—I know, but I can't help but feel as if I need to be wary for some reason, as if I don't deserve to be this content."

Now Amber snickered, "Oh baby, I love you so much, you're all I ever wanted and we've been through so much hell already. Don't we deserve some happiness too?"

Eduardo kissed her one last time before saying, "Just promise me Amber, if we ever find ourselves separated, Good God please remember that I will always love you."

Amber drew his head up from her neck and playfully kissed his eyes once more, "I promise."

"I love you."

"I love you, too," she declared, kissing his nose. "I'm famished—can we eat now? Do they actually serve food on this island?"

# AMBER

As long I could remember, I always knew something special was going to happen to me. When I was ten, I would cling onto that small hope that no matter how bad a day I was having, there was still something gigantic to expect just around the corner...

I'm no longer waiting.

The year I met my first husband, Victor Sanchez was also the year I met the love of my life, his older brother, Eduardo. I'll always remember that day because that was the day when my life turned upside down. Emotions I never knew existed were introduced and from thereon in, my life would never be the same.

I recalled having just met Victor's parents, Rosalba and Fabrizio and they were larger than life, a sweet, affectionate couple who showered their relatives with love and devotion. The Sanchez Family was such a tight-knit group with such strong convictions and I longed to be one of them having come from a family of regular divorce. Eduardo had been visiting his parents just out of Harvard law school and was one thrilling persona. His good fortune oozed out of his pores and I couldn't help but gawk at him at our initial meeting. And, oh God was he ever gorgeous! Good Lord, he was perfect. Every woman, not only me was mesmerized by him just standing there. He had been something else that day and I went home that night—the night Victor had proposed to me—a little overwhelmed not only by the memorable day of meeting his parents, family and being proposed to, but by experiencing chemistry I never thought existed.

Over the years, I thought I would go insane thinking that I'd never be able to quench my eagerness of wanting to be near him. Never in my wildest dreams would I have imagined that he had been feeling the very same thing. Come to think of it, there wasn't a moment I recall that whenever I was at a family gathering, Eduardo wasn't right by my side. We had this mysterious connection, him and I; a baffling longing of wanting a void to be fulfilled. But, oh God, how my emotions were tortured by just being around him! All I wanted to do was touch him when I saw him at those family gatherings. And to be brutally honest, temptation sucks. Pining away for someone also sucks. Your emotions go haywire, you feel like you can't breathe, you don't want to eat and your heart is all twisted. All you want to do is just be with that person and it kills you every day because you can't.

Eduardo and I didn't become lovers for nearly ten years, in fact, we were friends first and maybe that's how it should have been. Knowing the timeline and the outcome of our affair, I would have done things differently though. I just wanted to hold him, hug him, kiss him, lay on him, get naked and have him inside of me— all day long! Yes, it was obsessive, yes, it was immoral, but I couldn't ignore what my body kept telling me. We weren't related, we had no blood ties—he just happened to be my husband's older brother. To be attracted to your brother-in-law...Why was that so taboo?

There were no good reasons behind my fascination with Eduardo Sanchez, just like there are no good reasons behind a cat's appeal to catnip.

How do you explain the unexplainable? I was young; I only had one other boyfriend other than Victor and married right out of high school. How was I supposed to know how sexual attraction would affect me? Even at work, when I first started working at Eduardo's law firm, when he would walk passed my desk; my heart would do flip-flops. I never got any work done; his body and his face would always preoccupy my thoughts and definitely overpower my work load. It got so bad I would oftentimes cry in my car on my way home on the freeway and wipe away my tears as soon as I pulled into the garage so Victor wouldn't notice. I wished I were always somewhere else and constantly with him until the night Eduardo confessed his true mind-set.

Unbelievable...I was in total disbelief that he had been feeling the very same way? All those years I had been attracted to him, desiring his lips on mine, Eduardo had desired my lips on his?

I feel very lucky right now. I know I tried to commit suicide and I know now by going through a lot of therapy that I should have thought through my pain. But at the time, I wasn't thinking clearly and I don't know how else to explain those horrible moments of wanting to take my own life and I don't want to make excuses for what I did, but you don't think; all you see is the pain and the throbbing piled high on top of further misery whenever you think of who caused you that torture. I just wanted to end it, more than that; I wanted to teach him a lesson. The man was damn spoiled, Eduardo had always been spoiled, always getting what he wanted and what I wanted didn't matter. I wanted him to leave his wife (my sister-in-law, Leticia) for me. If he had truly loved and cared about me like he was constantly confessing, then why wasn't he willing to get a divorce? I was willing to leave Victor and my kids for him, why wasn't Eduardo willing to change direction for me?

Was it really his family convictions?  Was it his pride?  Or was it just him being a little overindulged?

So at that point, I just didn't care; I wanted to end it all.  I hated being the other woman; hated feeling dirty because I was a cheater and the only way I was going to cleanse myself, was to wash it all away, to stop it and that's just what I tried to do.

And I really don't remember all that much about that day.  All I remember is Eduardo and I fighting in the hotel room, me ripping off his gold chain and then seeing **RED**.  The next thing I remember is waking up in a white hospital bed and looking into the baby-blue scrub's of a friendly nurse smiling down at me.  I couldn't believe it when the doctor's explained to me that I had been in a coma for nearly sixteen months!  Sixteen months?  Good Lord, I was never meant to wake up; all I still wanted was just to end it—why did someone save me?  Turned out, it was my mother who found me.  My mother...of all people, the one and only family member that I thought was just as selfish as Eduardo did a maternal act.

I thought I was dead, I should have died, but then the more days I woke up with the sun in my face, the more I wanted to live!  I was given a second chance to change things, make amends and make life better for me.

Dr. Dirk Hayward was a Godsend.  He was a very caring man and the only man I was able to talk to or willing to speak with lacking being afraid and he helped me see the negativity of my past and how to turn it in to something positive.

Right now I have a progressive attitude, I feel bliss and I have never felt more fulfilled.  I feel as if I am walking on air or in a cloud of happiness, I feel loved, secure and warm and actually feel like I did die and went to Heaven.

# CHAPTER **THREE**

By slow degrees, Amber woke up before sunlight. Her heart was racing and her adrenaline pumped through her veins anxiously. Since leaving Fiji and her cloud nine state, it had been the first real night she and her latest husband had slept together throughout the night—she wasn't used to it. What she was used to was being at the Palm Desert Treatment Center in a twin bed with starched white sheets that smelled like bleach, **that** she was used to; with pampered treatment, round the clock nurses and Dr. Hayward, who she could always count on to listen to her insecurities and when she felt restless and confused as she did so now. But...**why**? She had absolutely everything she's ever wanted...a man who adored her, spoiling her to the point where his arms were her blanket and the long length of his body had been some source of bedding, but what was this new feeling of foreboding? Like the boogie man was about to pop out from nowhere and frighten her to the point where she would have to wake up from this wondrous dream. The fear felt like foreshadowing and the foreshadowing felt somewhat like a test... a great big test and she was afraid of making a mistake.

She looked over at her husband sleeping soundly. Good Lord, he was beautiful asleep! Like someone had posed him, he was on his back with one arm looped around on his head, she wanted to hug him, kiss him, dive into his chest, swim in his essence, love—fondle him, adore him, praise his glory, but instead she started to weep she was so overwhelmed with emotion and sprung out of bed and found herself outside on the balcony to get some fresh air.

Amber stood over by the edge overlooking the ocean. She still couldn't believe she was even there! This was her home now and this was her new life. It was as if she went to sleep one night with an old husband and an old family and woke up in the morning to a new husband with a new family. Like some strange episode of the Twilight Zone: Walking through one door and stepping into a new dimension, one switch to the other, effortlessly with no one to tell her that it had all been wrong. She had awakened up from her coma only to be introduced to a new world, a state-of-the-art frontier and she wasn't too sure she could handle it and Eduardo had taken care of everything. What a control freak he was! After he whisked her away on a private jet to Fiji, he brought her back to Pacific Palisades in California to present her with their new residence; an exquisite five bedroom, four baths Mediterranean home with a stunning lagoon themed pool, playhouse and play area with swing-set and sandbox for her son and tennis court for Amber. A fricken **tennis court...**and she didn't even play tennis, but Eduardo did, and she knew he always wanted one. She guessed she would have to take tennis lessons just to keep up with the pro.

Amber loved the feeling of being sheltered and taken care of. All her life she searched for someone to make her feel complete and now she's seized it. Her Father Figure had taken care of her needs and she no longer had to worry about her financial future and recalled the conversation she had a couple of nights ago discussing the very same thing. They were in the middle of eating dinner when Amber announced she wanted to go back to work...

"What?"

"I think it's time for me to look for a new job."

"Amber, what about Peyton?" He asked, looking over at his son eating his food skillfully with a child's fork.

"He'll be fine. He's got my mother and Mrs. Lopez to look after him while I'm at work."

"You don't have to work you know."

"What do you mean?"

"Do you think you need to contribute financially to this marriage?"

"Well sure, don't I? I mean, look at this house Eduardo, it must have cost you a fortune!"

Eduardo guffawed and rolled up his napkin. "Amber, let me tell you something. Last year, I grossed over ten million. This year, maybe even fifteen. I've managed my money very well and have investments in both real estate and stocks. Philip and Martin offered to make me partner, which would only bring in additional income. You never need to work again sweetheart. So by marrying me, you've become a woman of leisure."

Good Lord, she couldn't believe it! Being able to purchase anything her heart so desired? What would she buy first? A new car, new clothes, furniture, jewelry, china...then she started thinking about all the practical things she would need for the new home...A washer and dryer? No, Eduardo had taken care of that. A refrigerator—nope, he had taken care of that too. Flat screen TV's in every room of the house? Nope, he bought those too! What the hell could she contribute to this new marriage anyhow?

She was beginning to panic when she felt her husband's arms drape around her shoulders in a warm loving embrace.

"My bed is cold. Come back to sleep."

Amber closed her eyes and felt Eduardo's lips on her neck, kissing her with feather-like ardor up and down her crux. "I will in a second."

"What are you doing out here?" He murmured to her, continually grazing her neck with his velvety lips. Amber turned around within his arms. "What do you love about me? I mean, really, why would you love someone like me if I can't be a factor to this marriage?"

Eduardo stared at Amber as if she had three eyes in the center of her head, "A factor? Are you talking about going back to work again? Amber, you know how I feel about the matter."

Amber wrapped her arms around his neck, "I know, but I still want to do something in this marriage. What can I do?"

"You can contribute by continuing to make your husband deliriously happy, that's what you can do."

Amber, for some stupid reason, **did not** like his answer. "I live to make you happy?"

Eduardo gave her a small kiss on her lips, "Amber, do you even realize how you make me feel?"

Amber gulped; her husband was about to cast out sonnets of love again. "I know you love me—"

"**Dear girl**...I love everything about you. I love that you're stubborn, I love that you keep me on my toes and stand up to my big ego and me. All my life Amber, I've had this dominant presence, intimidating men and dating women for the simple fact that they succumb to my leverage. But for once in my presumptuous life, someone has actually **conquered me**. I'm mush when I'm around you and I'm in heaven in your arms."

Amber's breath was taken away. She wrapped her arms around her husband's neck tighter and began to cry in his shoulder. Good Lord, she loved his man!

Amber ordered Chinese food one night and setup Peyton's dinner with Mrs. Lopez and sent him off with her early. Eduardo came home and wanted to go out to eat like they usually did on Fridays, when Amber spat out unexpectedly, "Let's stay in."

Eduardo had always been spoiled and wanted to do what he wanted to do, and usually got his way and nodded his head "no".

"We're spending too much money eating out," Amber softly voiced, grabbing his yoke and leading him upstairs to his surprise. "I want to stay home and have you all to myself."

Mrs. Lopez helped her set up the terrace outside and it was a gorgeous evening with the waves from the ocean in the background as their music and the sea breeze rising up from the ocean as their aroma.

Eduardo was pleased and gave his wife a smirk while he sat down to eat a plate of pot-stickers, ginger beef and lo mein.

After dinner, Amber put in a Kenny G CD and they slowly danced and swayed to the romantic music.

"Where did you learn to dance?" Amber asked Eduardo as if they never danced before. "You lead me like you know exactly what you're doing, like you've taken lessons before."

"At dance clubs when I was younger," he nodded, "And the rest just naturally."

Amber rolled her eyes and felt Eduardo's hands roaming her lower back and then down to her bottom. She pulled apart from him and ran her hands up his chest.

"I've never wanted to touch a man the way I want to touch you," she revealed in a seductive timbre.

Eduardo nearly lost it and slid both hands down to her derriere and squeezed each cheek into his formation.

Amber was instantly breathless. "How do you do that?" She respired, catching her breath.

"Do what?" He rejoined in her ear, kissing the back of her earlobe and continuing to sway her to the romantic music.

"Make a woman want you."

"Skill," he let go without a hint of shame.

Amber lightly kissed him on his lips, "You are so bad...but I'm so glad **you're all mine**."

Eduardo grabbed the back of her hair then opened her up mouth with his tongue. Amber collected him with her wide-open mouth accepting all he had to offer.

Eduardo broke apart from her immediately, "I'm finished swaying on the balcony, want to dance in bed?"

Amber nearly started to hoot when Eduardo didn't even wait for her to answer and collected her up and ran with her body back to the bedroom.

# CHAPTER FOUR

Maria Lopez was turning fifty-seven this year. She never had any children and was married only once. But since the death of her husband, she felt lonely and unneeded and decided to become a caregiver. Having filled out job application after job application, she finally came across a friend of hers who had been a private nanny for a prevalent family in Beverly Hills and stroke up a conversation with the Latina in between the cucumber and the zucchini while at the grocery store. The woman told her about an agency that placed women like her in wealthy households on one condition – she needed to pass a series of qualifications: Good credit, fingerprinting, no histories of physical or mental abuse, alcohol free and a clear background check of any criminal history through the Department of Justice and she was in. **No problema**.

She met Mr. Sanchez through the placement agency when he was looking for a full-time live-in nanny and she moved in with them and had been Peyton's nanny since the day he was born. So of course she would feel a little overprotective of him, she loved that little boy as if he were her own and felt bad when Mrs. Sanchez (Amber) suddenly appeared after waking up from her coma.

Peyton never looked at his mother, nor asked to be near her and had no apparent bond with his natural birth parent. He oftentimes cried for Sheila Thomas, Peyton's grandmother, who stayed with Peyton when he was just a few months old, but, then moved out a few months later after Mrs. Sanchez arrived. But, nine times out of ten, Peyton felt most comfortable with Mrs. Lopez, and of course, his father.

'Mrs. Lopez' was what she liked to be called, and oftentimes brought Peyton outside in the backyard to play in the sand or swing on his swing set. Mrs. Sanchez would tag along, but would never really enforce her son to hug her or talk to her, even to be near her. Mrs. Lopez wondered about her motives, but soon found out after spending so much time alone with Mrs. Sanchez, that she seemed afraid—afraid of her own son's rejection? That's why she didn't push him to receive her so openly. Mrs. Sanchez would wait patiently until Peyton accepted her touch; acknowledge that she was his mother.


Mrs. Lopez was outside sitting next to Peyton while he scooped up sand with his plastic bucket. In the corner of her eye she noticed Mrs. Sanchez in the doorway, looking over at the two of them. Mrs. Lopez waved her hand to bring her over and Mrs. Sanchez began to walk toward Peyton playing.

Peyton instantly sprung to attention and noticed his mother walking toward him. Alarmed and frightened, he stood up and ran into Mrs. Lopez's reassuring arms.

Amber froze at the sight of her son running away from her advance and stared at Mrs. Lopez as she gently rubbed Peyton's black-haired head. Oh how she wished that were she!

Later, Amber tried again by offering him a toy but then Peyton ran toward Eduardo when he arrived through their front door. Peyton was totally at ease with his daddy and his daddy gave his son a big bear hug, unaware of the envy brewing in his wife.

"How was your day?" Eduardo asked his son, kneeling down so that he could meet him eye-to-eye.

"Fine daddy, how wa'ours?  Settle cases?"

Amber brought her hand up over her mouth and started to cry and ran up the winding staircase.

Eduardo gazed over quizzically at Mrs. Lopez as she just looked away indecisive.

"Peyton mehiò, come with me to change your clothes for bed," Mrs. Lopez asked the little boy, extending out her arm so that Peyton could take her hand.

Peyton gazed up at Mrs. Lopez, "OK nanny."

Eduardo shot a weird look at Mrs. Lopez and raised an eyebrow at her.

Mrs. Lopez was taken-back, what did he just call her?  "Peyton mehiò, what did you just say?"

"What does he usually call you?" Eduardo asked uncertain.

"Mrs. Lopez."

"The lady up-stwhere's told me to call her nanny," Peyton innocently responded.

Mrs. Lopez almost fainted at the endearment.  How nice of Mrs. Sanchez to ask her son to call her such a personal name.  For years now she often wondered if Mr. Sanchez ever considered her part of the family, and now, as tears swarmed her eyes, Peyton just proved how much he really cared.

"Well, you **are** the nanny," Eduardo winked at her. "But by those tears in your eyes, I'm thinking you're hoping it's a word for **grandma**."

Mrs. Lopez shushed him.  "Peyton mehiò, let's go upstairs and try to find the lady."

"Not before me," Eduardo halted her.  "Wait here, I'll call for you."

As soon as he made it upstairs, Eduardo found Amber on the bed crying.  He walked over to her and wrapped his arms around her shoulders and brought her in close. "What's wrong?"

"Your son doesn't even know me."

"My son? He's **ours** dear girl."

"Yah, you keep telling me that. But he doesn't even know me. He doesn't feel comfortable with me; he runs away from me at all the times—do you know how that makes me feel?"

Eduardo wiped the tears away from her face and kissed her lightly on her lips. "It's only been a couple of month's sweetheart, it will take some time. Peyton is a strong-willed boy. Just give it some time."

"I don't know if I can."

"Sure you can. We have all the time in the world." Eduardo stood up and motioned for Mrs. Lopez to bring Peyton upstairs and to his son's room. "Now, go and wash your face and get our son ready for bed. Mrs. Lopez has already started his bath."

Amber looked across from her husband. If this was going to work, then she would have to be adaptable. "OK."

A few minutes later, Amber filled the doorway to find Mrs. Lopez pulling Peyton's pajamas over his little tan body. He was a perfect interlock between Eduardo and her, taking after Eduardo physically, with black hair, hands, mouth like his mommy and green eyes, nose and skin tone like his daddy. Oh how she loved him so.

Amber noticed that Peyton was missing a button on his nightshirt, and inquired, "Peyton baby...would you come here?"

"No," he quickly said.

Amber rolled her eyes, "Come here Peyton, I'd like to button up your jammies."

Peyton hesitated and then slowly walked over to Amber. Looking down at her hands, Amber carefully fastened the open buttonhole on his pajama top.

"There now," she smiled, "You're all ready for bed."

"Would you weed me a stor-wee?" Peyton asked wide-eyed and innocent.

Amber almost expired from the familiarity in those green eyes. Amazing how she had never been this close up to him before where she could really view his eyes. She had always been able to study him from afar and now she had been given a great opportunity. Those were most definitely, his father's lashes and most definitely his father's hypnotic stare. Lord help those girls when he gets a little older. Amber gazed over at Eduardo who was filling the doorway now with his arms crossed, his legs crossed, smiling an adoring grin. "I sure would, but would you come sit next me?" Amber asked a stone-faced Peyton. "I don't like it when you sit so far away."

"Nanny says not to sit next to strang'weres."

Amber gazed down at the ground. Strangers? I guess she would be considered a stranger to him. Why would he have an instant connection with her anyhow? Birthing a child does not always make you an instant parent or give you an immediate connection—it took some desire, nourishing and a whole lotta love. The only adults Peyton has ever known were his grandmother, Eduardo and Mrs. Lopez. "Peyton, do you know what a mother is?"

Peyton walked over to his fake toy stethoscope and wrapped it around his shoulders and laid it down on his pajamas. "A mother is like a nurse, she takes care of babies."

"That's right Peyton," Amber agreed. "Do you know who I am?"

Peyton turned to look up at Mrs. Lopez first then back at Amber and quizzically stared at her. "You're my daddy's frwend."

Amber giggled, "Yes, I am your daddy's friend, but I'm also your mother. I'm your **mommy** Peyton."

Peyton continued to stare at the tall friendly lady he's been spending so much time with and he seemed confused, "My mommy?"

"Yes Peyton baby, I'm your mommy," Amber gushed, trying to hold back her tears. "And I love you very much."

Peyton walked over to Amber and placed his stethoscope on her chest. "Can I wisten to your heart...mommy?"

Tears streamed down Amber's face instantly and she leaned down to his level—wanting to grab him into her, hold him something fierce—but restrained herself and didn't want to break the comfortable bond she just created. "Like this?" She asked, sticking her chest out feeling deliriously happy.

Peyton cautiously placed the device in the middle of her shirt. "You have a hef-ee heart mommy; you don't need an oper-wation."

Amber wiped away her tears, "Thank goodness for that!"

Peyton was just about to walk away from her when Amber reached down and grabbed his little hand and brought his body into hers to give him a little hug. Peyton didn't hug her back but did allow her to give him a squeeze as he simply stared down at the carpet.

And Amber had to accept it. She accepted it because this was how it was for a while; this was how her life would be for the next few months until Peyton would be comfortable enough with her. She would have to be patient for a while and wait for that day to come, after all, like Eduardo said; they had all the time in the world now.

# CHAPTER FIVE

"She's here," Jackie Medina, Eduardo's Legal Assistant stated, closing the door behind her. She looked across at her boss. He had been going over a brief with his feet up on his desk when she popped in unannounced and he immediately placed them down within hearing her voice.

Eduardo laid down the brief first before saying, "Let her sit with the commoner's for a few more moments in the reception area. Let her reflect on what might have been."

Jackie smiled and agreed, "Yah, that'll teach her a lesson," she quipped, rolling her eyes disagreeing with him for now, "Sitting with the little people always makes me wanna reflect."

Eduardo gave her a condescending look of disapproval and Jackie simply raised her eyebrows and headed out the same way she came in. She could do that you know Jackie had been his assistant for nearly ten years. She had been assigned to him when he was initially hired and not once had she ever felt like pouncing on him. For the past five years, Jackie has had an unrequited love with Gordon Daggert, the other fine-looking attorney in the law firm. She was puttied around Gordon but with Eduardo, she felt more like his little sister and loved to tease him.

Eduardo gazed over at his digital clock then rolled his eyes. **The woman was early**, he thought. She could sit there for a few more minutes, he could make her wait. The last time she came in for an appointment, he was discussing her options on what to do about her agent of two years, who just happened to be her husband...and who just happened to have an affair with **her** assistant. She wanted to divorce him first, but then was arrested after her assistant found him dead at the foot of their bed. The spouse was always the first to suspect, and Eduardo was called in immediately by her publicist.

Imelda Yasmina Venezuela de Gómez aka "Yazmine" was a phenomenal pop singer imported from South America with a triple-platinum CD and five number one debut hits. She was at the peak of her popularity when the scandal hit. She didn't do it, she always claimed, and now Eduardo had to prove it. Oh, and there was one other little minor thing...she was a huge flirt. It had been rumored through the tabloids that she has had numerous lovers throughout her career and even some during her short two-year marriage to her agent. Yazmine didn't like hearing the word "no" and the day since she's been his client, Yazmine has also had the 'hots' for her Latin defense attorney. This is the reason why Eduardo made her cool down in the reception area, he didn't feel like being chased around his desk today—he just bought a new Armani suit.

She walked into his office in a low-cut dress and Eduardo's eyes immediately dropped to that region. He was, after all, a red-blooded American male—it was just in his nature.

"How's my favorite boy-toy?" Yazmine asked, making herself at home across from him on his sofa he had in his office.

Eduardo was about to go and sit back around his desk after greeting her when he noticed that she preferred to sit a little cozier and took her lead on a convenient chair across from her. "He's doing well," he confessed, thinking about Amber and their love-making just the night before. "He's doing **very** well."

Yazmine ate him up and down then crossed her legs to give him a view of her recent Miami tan through her slit on her leather mini skirt. Yazmine misread his stare and didn't skip a beat and commented on that sensual look of his, "In no doubt you are..."

Later that afternoon, Amber felt uneasy at home knowing her husband was having a meeting with that she-devil. Just the other day at the hair salon, Amber had picked up a magazine with an entire section on **'Yazmine'** and how famous she was and how the paparazzi constantly stalked her to the point where she had to hire a few bodyguards and entourage. She was with them, she claimed, when her husband was killed and she was blaming her assistant for his death. Amber didn't like her...of course, she was a **blond**...and, of course, she was **beautiful**...and, of course, she had a **nice rack** and Eduardo loved to look at blonds who were beautiful with nice racks. Those used to be his preferred women of choice and had Amber really tamed the once promiscuous tiger? Had he really changed? Had a tiger really maintained his stripes?

Amber hadn't been jealous of other women in his life since the day they were married, but with this one, she felt apprehension and couldn't understand why.

Amber was just about to call Eduardo at the office to see how his meeting went with Yazmine when Amber browsed by the kitchen and found Mrs. Lopez making food for her son. "Mrs. Lopez, I can make lunch for Peyton, you don't have to do that."

"I insist, Mrs. Sanchez, I've been making sure Peyton has had a good meal since the day he was born."

Amber felt her blood beginning to boil, "But I'm his mother Mrs. Lopez, and I am quite capable of making a peanut butter and jelly sandwich."

"Peanut butter and jelly?" Mrs. Lopez nodded her head, "No—no, little Peyton must eat chopped chicken like his father."

Amber fumed, "No, he doesn't. I'm taking over now and Peyton is going to grow up normal—unlike his spoiled father."

"Are you insulting your own husband?"

"No one knows Eduardo Sanchez more than I do, he's arrogant, he's difficult, he's brilliant, but he's spoiled."

Mrs. Lopez nodded her head again, "You will take full responsibility if Mr. Sanchez is unhappy with Peyton's nutrition then?"

Amber rolled her eyes. The woman was insulting her again! "Yes, full responsibility."

"Very well then, I will see to the other house duties."

What other house duties? Amber had already walked all over the Goddamn house and found that there was not one inch of dust or grime, dirty clothes, dishes, an unmade bed or a bathroom unclean throughout the whole entire area! The whole house was military dirt free and it was making her crazy from the sheer boredom of having nothing to do! "Very well," Amber mocked, watching Mrs. Lopez exit out of the kitchen.

Amber then began opening up the cupboards trying to figure out where the hell the peanut butter went when she came across a cabinet full of liquor and closed it up immediately; didn't give a second glance until she hesitated for a second and then reopened it. Amber after that took out the Vodka bottle directly in front of her and poured herself a small glass.

Wow, how comforting it was to relax her nerves. Amber began to recall all the endless nights when she couldn't sleep, or tried to find a reason to avoid sleeping with Victor. She was involved with Eduardo back then and she didn't want Victor to touch her so she found out by drinking, she discovered the escape and finally an answer. Amber was one of the drinkers who, if drank the right amount, would transform physically into another person all together. She was suddenly unsure about her husband's roving eye and that housekeeper slash nanny was nothing but difficult lately, and Amber continued to pour herself drinks until she realized she had drank half the bottle.

Later, Eduardo came home to find Mrs. Lopez at the dining-room table rearranging the flowers. "Where's Mrs. Sanchez?"

"She's been up in her room for half the day."

"Where's Peyton?"

"Your mother-in-law was by here earlier and asked if he could attend her to the park."

"Oh," Eduardo let go, ascending the staircase and noticing that the door to their room had been closed.

He opened it up to find Amber asleep in their bed. But it was only six-thirty! Amber usually greeted him at the door with her arms wide open, kissing him excitedly. He was not used to her halting their routine. "Amber?"

Amber moaned.

Eduardo walked over to her lying there. She looked...drunk. Her face was smashed against the mattress; her lips were spread out in a funny widened fish mouth expression. Eduardo shook his head, lifted her feet up and took off her shoes. "Amber...I'm home."

Amber moaned another time.

She **had** been drinking. What the hell for? Eduardo slapped his wife's bottom with one quick stroke.

Amber flinched and sprung to attention. "Ouch! What the fuck?"

"Have you been drinking?"

Amber tried to open her inebriated eyes and squinted at her husband. Her senses came back to her in full force. "Just a little bit," she explained, pinching her fingers to show him just how much.

"Why? You don't drink, what's wrong?"

"I had a rough day," she said, wiping her plastered hair away from her face.

Eduardo had never seen her like this before. Her eyes had suddenly changed. The alteration in her was almost immediate. Her hazel eyes transformed from light brown to a dingy black. Her face went pale, she was almost white. Her usual pink hue was gone, vanished, erased over by the intoxication. He was so turned off by her appearance he couldn't believe the mutation in her.

Amber went for her husband and started to kiss him, but Eduardo held her back. He was suddenly disgusted with what he saw and conveyed, "Stop it Amber, I'm tired, I'm going to take a shower."

Amber let go of him instantly and watched wide-eyed as he walked away from her. Eduardo had **never-ever** rejected her touch before! Was it the singer? Was it really work? Was he really tired? What was it?

Amber suddenly was in disbelief, and then without warning, she had a craving for another drink.

# Chapter SIX

In the middle of the night, Amber had a sudden burst of mother's intuition. Her child was hurting. She sat up and listened to the various sounds across the hushed night. Eduardo was whizzing in his sleep, his nose snoring away. So much for being faultless, another flaw she could use as ammunition for a rainy day. Amber closed her eyes again, maybe she was imagining it; the wind, rustling through the leaves on the trees outside, the ocean beyond, the waves pushing up against the current, splashing and tumbling over and over...then a small faint sound...the cry of child...**Peyton?**

Amber darted out of bed and ran toward her son's room. The light from the moon streamed through his windowpane. She focused on him instantly; Peyton was rolling on top of his bed, whimpering and crying and Amber ran over to him directly and grabbed him into her arms.

Peyton immediately stopped crying when he felt secured by an adult's warm arms around him. He was safe now, the nightmare could end and he wrapped his little arms around that other person; unaware that it was his mother.

Still holding him within her arms, Amber walked over to the nearby rocking chair and sat down and carefully rocked her child within her arms. She caressed his head, his back and then rubbed him over and over until he felt completely safe.

"Mommy's here baby," she whispered to him, rocking and swaying her child until she felt his body loosen from her comforting words. "Mommy won't let anything happen to you, the monsters are all gone now, mommy's here baby...You're safe now Peyton, you're safe with mommy."

Amber's heart swarmed with love at this point. It was the second time she ever got to hold her child. The first day was when Eduardo presented him to Amber when she had awakened from her unconscious state back at the Palm Desert Treatment Center. Peyton had been asleep and hadn't noticed the exchange of arms that had taken place.

Amber continued to rock her son as the moonlight shifted around in the windowsill from the wind outside. She continued kissing him in his sleepy dreamy state and was so grateful for this little time alone with him where he allowed her to fully hold him without any interruption, hesitation or Mrs. Lopez. She kissed Peyton on the top of his head and caressed and held him near. She didn't realize how much she truly loved this little boy until that moment; he was her miracle, an additional benefit to hers and Eduardo's already full love and she was so grateful to have him.

Peyton instantly fell back to sleep, feeling secure, feeling the love and warmth from his mother; and Amber closed her eyes and thanked God for him. She never asked for him in the first place, never thought she was allowed to have such a special gift, but here he was and she was so indebted that he was now with her and thanked the Lord again for creating him for her to love and share with the man she would forever care for.

Amber reopened her eyes and fathomed in the darkness—her husband? He doesn't interrupt them and watched her silently as she rocked the chair back and forth in the middle of the night with their child in her arms.

Eduardo smiled inwardly. He had awakened up to go to the bathroom and noticed his wife went missing. He stumbled over to the balcony but she wasn't there. He roamed the downstairs, she wasn't there either. He never thought she would go into Peyton's room to wake him up, but when he entered the doorway, he stood back in the shadows while he watched Peyton cling to his mother for reassurance.

There was the woman he would die for; holding the son he always wanted and he recalled the day Leticia (his ex-wife) told him that she was pregnant for the second time. He didn't believe her...he hadn't been sleeping with her, unless she had been cheating on him, how else could she have gotten pregnant? It turned out that she wasn't with child, it was a false alarm, but Amber was.

Eduardo remembered when he found out from the nurse at the county hospital, where Amber was taken to that she had been expectant. He was in disbelief and so uncertain, but elated at the same time. He was happy for her and hoped that her pregnancy would go well and went to see Victor (his brother) to give him the good news. Eduardo would be the one to tell him that they were expecting another child, when Victor laid down the ugly truth ...it couldn't have been his baby, Victor confessed. He wasn't sleeping with her as well; in fact, Amber and he hadn't made love for nearly a year. So, that meant...it was Eduardo's?! Eduardo was the father?

Eduardo was over the moon and immediately ran to Sheila, hoping that he could make amends with her as well and it worked. Sheila immediately responded to Eduardo and with this new baby on the way, connected them all in more ways than one. He was no longer the **'bad guy'** in the relationship, he was the **'soon to be father'** and positive attention was given to him straight away.

And oh how he loved the thought of having a child with Amber! **If she only woke up**, he often thought. They could be a blissful, happy family, those were his aspirations now. His once incessant need of being the best, the smartest, the sharpest attorney known to mankind unraveled to becoming the best dad ever.

Silent days and nights with Amber now at the Palm Desert Treatment Center turned in to nail-biting months of waiting and wondering if Amber's womb would either accept or deny their unborn child. She was in a comatose state, unresponsive and unaware of the marvel growing inside her. She was one of just a handful of women who have been recorded pregnant while being comatose and the doctors all told Eduardo to expect a negative outcome, that Amber would not survive the trauma on her body if she ever did give birth. Oh, how that tore him to pieces! There was now a terrible decision he had to make. The doctors gave him a choice to either terminate the pregnancy and give Amber a chance or let the gestation developed naturally, but not to term. Terminate the pregnancy? Eduardo thought about it all of five seconds and the answer was no. In his heart, he knew, somehow he knew that Amber would awake and her love for him still intact. But with that decision, the doctors all told Eduardo to expect the worse, bear down and accept the obvious, that Amber's past medical history was unfavorable and therefore, the pregnancy would never bear a healthy child. If it would even make it to a full nine months...and Peyton made it to seven and a half. He was tiny, premature and needed medical care instantaneously. He was in an incubator for the first three months of his life until he gained enough weight to be on his own. And the doctors all told Eduardo, to expect the worse, bear down and expect the obvious, that Peyton would probably suffer mental incapacities, birth defects or poorer from here on in, but here he was...normal, growing by leaps and bounds and ever so smart!  He was a bright child and loving, astute and Eduardo could have never imagined that this would be the happy outcome for all three of them; his wife, waking up nine months later and his little boy, healthy and thriving, learning other languages, curious about medicine and now knowing his mother.

How lucky could one man be?

# EDUARDO

Persistence breeds determination, and determination creates boldness.  So when a man owns his assertiveness, perceived as being accomplished with his intellect, then its deliberate self-assurance, arrogance and occasionally, conceit...

And what does this all mean, everything once—and not so important anymore.

College, graduate school and becoming an associate in a prestigious Westside law firm have all been predestined and under my control....women at all times were my weakness.

Handsome, gorgeous, beautiful, charming, attractive, good-looking, seductive, interesting and tempting, these were the labels that I've had to grow up with.  School was easy; college was a breeze even graduating from Harvard was uncomplicated.  Girls, dating and maintaining a relationship had always been a difficult mission.

The day I met Amber, I was supposed to meet another girl after checking in at my parents' home.  They were throwing a party for me, a barbeque with all my relatives to help celebrate my coming home and graduating Harvard.  I had a one-track mind back then; family to me was not all that essential, only girls and my aspirations to get to the top.  So meeting my little brother's

46

new girlfriend was just another fleeting duty until her eyes crashed into mine. To this day I cannot explain it. What happened to me in that moment, I felt like another world had been exposed, a mysterious one, full of new challenges and innovative possibilities. I said hello to her, but Amber didn't return my greeting, she just kept staring, which I was used to, but I kept my sole focus on her; that I was not familiar with. I watched them walk away, my brother and his new girlfriend and I not only observed them walking away, I envied my brother's arms around her waist. Damn, that blew my mind. I had never been covetous of anyone, especially my own brother and I had never been that drawn to a woman in all my life and I've dated a lot of fascinating stunning females. Gorgeous, Top Ten's, Playboy worthy and elite model's; only the prettiest girl would do and I was always very selective and never alone. So meeting Amber that day was probably the worst thing that could have happened to me.

And the best.

I was in love with her.

I guess you could say (and I hate to admit it even to this very day) thirteen years later that I fell in love at first sight. I trusted my own feelings in that I would never allow myself to fully fall for any female. Eduardo Sanchez doesn't fall in love with anyone. I hated to feel chaotic and confused and females play with a male's heart and I was never fully prepared for that. I always held the upper hand; if the female got too close to me then I always found a way to let them down gently. Always the winner; never the loser but on that day of the barbecue, I had lost my fuckin mind.

I couldn't sleep, I couldn't eat—I could barely concentrate at work! Good God, I had never been that sporadic. All I wanted to do was touch her, just once, hold her in my arms and test the theory that it was only my curiosity and that I really didn't need her or require to be by her side; but even that failed and once my investigation was met, my lust took over. Amber was my target, she was my food and I couldn't exist if I wasn't able to be near her day or night.

Good God, I hated those days. Hated knowing I was one of those fools you read about who had been besotted by another human being. One of those stupid idiots I used to make fun of at night clubs or on TV, even at work; watch them crawling on their knees, getting their hearts broken in two. I wasn't **him**, I couldn't be him, but the more I thought about her, the more I was evolving into that moron and there was nothing I could do about it. Amber was always on my mind until I finally couldn't take it anymore and I had to taste her, had to feel her body next to mine, had to be inside her and I wasn't going to settle for just one time. Once our affair began, I knew I wasn't going to be able to stop it. Amber was all I ever wanted and I didn't want the feeling of euphoria to end. Whenever we were together it was like magic; I had never felt so finished, she was like my drug of choice and I was so obsessed.

I'm in love with her; **still** in love with Amber.

And when she gave me that choice on that horrible day, I wished to God I would have told her that I would have left Leticia. Always wished I could go back in time and relive those moments when we were in heat and she was in anguish over my lack of common sense. I would have left Leticia in a heartbeat; I just didn't want to hurt my family. It was reasonable, even to this day, it is still understandable. Amber said she would have done anything for me and I was such an amateur at love, the one test where I was supposed to come out the winner, I lost again; and nearly lost the love of my life.

Sixteen months of living hell was my punishment for not yielding, sixteen months of anguish and torture of not knowing if she was going to succumb to her comatose state or wake up and forgive me.

I literally fell to my knees at work when Dr. Hayward called and told me that Amber had finally woken up. Closed my eyes and vowed that I would never be that dumb. Lesson learned, it would never happen to me again.

# CHAPTER SEVEN

*One Year Later*

"Oh, I hate going to these things," Amber grumbled, straightening out her evening gown.

They were at one of the several investor slash shareholder fund raising events that they had been given an invitation to. Eduardo had gotten real good at investing his well-earned money and built his name and holding company up by tenfold and the parties were just fancy excuses to help celebrate everyone having made good ventures.

"Stop whining," Eduardo hissed at her, gazing around the room for a familiar face; when he spotted one of his investing partners across the span, he quickly added, "You look great, by the way." He leaned into her and gave her a soft kiss on her forehead, "Now there's Anthony Rivera, you know, the investor I told you about last month?"

Amber gazed out toward her husband's line of direction; she didn't see anyone who looked familiar. "Yes, but no, what does he look like?"

"That's right, you two never met," Eduardo realized, getting ready to go over and greet him, "Wait at the bar, I'll go and bring him over."

Bring him over? Wait at the bar? Amber then rolled her eyes and looked over at the elongated mahogany with all the shiny bottles calling out her name. She did what she was told and walked over to have a sit. She waited all but five seconds before the bartender asked her what she wanted to drink. A martini sounded good and the bartender handed her something pink. Two glasses later and she was feeling mighty fine and glanced out at the crowd and didn't see Eduardo anywhere. How dare he abandon her there!

Amber was just about to leave her seat when her view was suddenly clouded over by a black tuxedo tie.

"You're beautiful," she heard the tie say.

Amber then raised her eyes to his face and thought pretty much the same thing. The man was terribly good-looking; she realized immediately and felt a stab of guilt of admitting the observation. Amber just smiled, "Thank you."

"Please tell me you came here alone."

Amber smiled again and looked down at her crossed legs. The tip of her knee had been exposed along with her long dark tanned legs. At that moment she did feel beautiful and looked up at the stranger and into his eyes. They were brown, but mesmerizing, hypnotic; he was also Latin and very, very pleasant on **her** eyes. "No," she nodded, grinning again, only sweetly this time, "I'm here with my husband."

The man let out an apparent sigh and tilted his head from one side still admiring the view. "Lucky man," he said, about to walk away only to be cornered by Amber's husband.

"So you met?" Eduardo asked sternly, shifting looks from his wife and then to his investment partner.

At that moment, Amber felt a shiver go up and down her spine. She couldn't determine whether it was the alcohol or the new arrival's apparent physical chemistry. She felt an immediate connection with this stranger and couldn't understand why.

Amber then stood up from her perched position and stood up next to her husband, "Um, no honey, we haven't met."

The gentlemen beamed and displayed his pearly white teeth and Amber nearly expired at that moment. Eduardo's business partner had a polished smile and his eyes lit up when he exposed that grin which only seemed to enhance his magnetic appearance. She was so drawn to this man, it frightened her.

"So this is Mrs. Sanchez?" The man simply relayed, putting two and two together.

Amber looked shyly down at the ground first before extending out her hand for him to shake.

"Tony Rivera, this is my wife, Amber," Eduardo said next, ignoring their bizarre intense moments.

Anthony Rivera, aka Tony to his very intimate friends, took Amber's hand and instead of shaking it like any normal person would do, felt the impulse to kiss the back of her knuckles like a gentlemen of the eighteenth century. He had been so taken by her; he rolled his eyes only to close them because he just made an absolute fool of himself in front of Eduardo and probably pay for it financially later. He didn't want to come off as looking like he was trying too hard, but he was never one to steal another man's wife. Don't get him wrong, Tony has had numerous lovers over the years, all brunettes and his female of choice. Tall, stunningly beautiful with dark or auburn hair and Mrs. Sanchez would have been some trophy. He had just broken up with his live-in girlfriend of seven years; Cara, that was her name, they even had a daughter together, but after they lost her to leukemia, they coasted apart in depression and Tony's been drifting ever since to one girl to the next. Never wanting to be alone, he tried not to look too desperate but the next few ladies would always stay weeks at a time and grab a few baubles on their way out. His business was booming however and Tony decided to concentrate on making more money and met Eduardo Sanchez through a mutual friend of theirs. Deciding to go into trade with him, he started with a few short-term investments and turned out that those minor interim investments converted into rather large funds and figured being in business with Eduardo Sanchez was a no-brainer, and Eduardo was of equal mind; he was a smart cat and Tony fed off of him and his ideas. Eduardo had a great eye for finance and Tony would throw in his two cents and the both of them would often come out on top. Eduardo would frequently talk about his wife but Tony would always try and change the subject. Eduardo was always so upbeat and seemed too happy, even for him and Tony only wanted to wallow in his misery. He needed some serious help; he needed to get laid.

Eduardo gave a quick look over at his wife at that moment and saw her embarrassment, or maybe, her enchantment? "So Tony, the ink has already dried," he jokingly put out turning away from Amber, "There really is no need to score points with the misses."

Amber then wrapped her arm around her husband's forearm and plainly said, "Nice to meet you Mr. Rivera. My husband's told me nothing but good things about you."

Tony beamed and then shoved his hands down his front pant pockets. "It's Tony," he offered, making the mistake of dropping his eyes down to Amber's diamond necklace she had hanging from a chain that conveniently laid on top of her breasts inside her V-shaped gown. It seemed to captivate him. "I have nothing bad to say about him either," he just said, clearing his throat and raising his eyes back up to hers.

Eduardo scanned his partner's stance and immediately picked up on his attraction to his wife and decided now would be a good time to end the night. He would deal with his colleague one on one and on another day; tonight was just too close for comfort. "It was nice to see you Tony," Eduardo hastily laid out leading Amber away, "Call me tomorrow and we'll discuss what we talked about earlier, you know, about Long Beach?"

Tony met eyes with Eduardo first before resting his glare on his wife. "I'll be at the office all day," he voiced, giving Amber a small smile. "It was finally nice to meet you Mrs. Sanchez."

Amber smiled back, "Nice to have finally met you too, Mr. Rivera."


That night, Amber came home a little intoxicated, not only by the two martinis she had drank earlier, but from meeting Eduardo's new business partner, Anthony Rivera. Why was she so attracted to him at any rate? She had a man! The man of her **dreams**, so why was this total stranger so out of the ordinary?

"Turn around," she heard him say.

Amber blinked out of her fantasy and over at her husband. He had already discarded his body of his jacket, shirt, tie and pants, was wearing only is boxer shorts and a smile. "Why?"

"So I can unzip you," he grinned, grabbing her by the shoulders.

Amber felt her body twirl around and Eduardo's hands fondle at her backside when her dress suddenly dropped to the floor and warm, eager hands inched their way up towards her breasts from behind. She arched her back to receive him and his touch, his lips on her neck and without warning, his erection in her buttocks. She didn't want to do it like that, not tonight and turned around to meet his tongue and wrapped her arms around his shoulders, leading their bodies toward the bed.

He took the direction and lay on top of her instantly trying to find a home for his pleasure and Amber opened up her legs to welcome him in as Eduardo glided amid her, driving his high point home. Amber reached up to his neck and face and watched in mystification as his eyes turned brown...they were **brown**, his face had altered into Anthony Rivera's and Amber shut her eyes to ponder on this illusion that left her heated in the first place and felt her lions pulsate from the wonderful, concentrated orgasm that this stranger was able to stir up. It had been the first time she ever fantasized about another man while making love to Eduardo.

And that was downright scary.

# CHAPTER **EIGHT**

Occasionally Philip Aldridge, Eduardo's boss, asked him to meet the new associate when one was hired into the law firm. Get a feel for the person behind the resume; grill the new attorney on their background and dedication to the law. Eduardo was great at grilling; very good at excavating someone's hidden character to the surface and glad to do so.

But the moment she walked into his office—he knew he was in trouble. Stacey Somers, formerly, **Stacey Mitchell** had been the virgin that got away.

Stacey Mitchell was his high school girlfriend, also his vice president; a position held under him when he was the senior class president and Eduardo always wished that she was beneath him physically.

Stacey was a devoted Christian back in high school and held off for marriage. Bringing each other to a sizzling stage, but the girl would never fully succumb. Eduardo was always left limited and frustrated from Stacey not giving him what he really wanted; so by being young, he broke it off immediately to go and search for a girl who would. He vowed that he would never allow another female to yank the reigns of convictions like this girl once did. He knew he had broken her heart; several of her friends at school would corner him and deliver him letters that she had written. Inside, Stacey had poured her heart out and confessed that she was a virgin and that God had wanted her to wait to give her husband her virginity. She let him know that she was in love with him and if he wanted her to wait, she promised she would never allow another boy to touch her ever again until they were married. Good God, she was willing to **save** herself for him? Eduardo was just a kid, barely eighteen and didn't want to hold that kind of responsibility; didn't want to know he had that kind of control. He cut it off immediately and found a cheap girlfriend and Stacey left school a couple of months later, claiming to further her education at a Christian school up in Northern California.

Stacey Somers at present hadn't changed much; petite curvy figure with natural platinum blond hair, sparkling cobalt eyes with wet lips begging to be kissed. He was not only shocked to see her walk in; she had taken his very breath away...and that hadn't happened to him in a very long time.


Stacey froze within seeing him. **Eduardo Sanchez?** She hadn't seen him in over twenty years! Oh why didn't anyone tell her he was employed at the firm? She heard through the grapevine that he was some powerful high-priced defense attorney working on the Westside, but she never believed he'd be an associate at the firm she just got hired at! Eduardo was still handsome as ever as she felt her heart drop down to the pit of her stomach. He still had those penetrating green eyes, followed by that heavenly sculpted face of his. She remembered she fell in love with the good-looking boy back in high school, but now, she could **really** fall head over heels for the attractive successful man. His prominence, his sophistication and his elegance tied together with his irrefutable sex appeal was a lethal combination. Just knowing that he was once interested in her made the test all the more worthwhile.

Stacey tried to contain herself from being so pleased within finding her seat across from him and smiled internally and thanked the Lord for giving her a second chance to win him back. They were high school sweethearts, she had recalled and very much in love, so she thought. She had lost to his presidency back in high school and didn't really know of him until she had to report for student council. Their initial meeting was transfixing, in that she had never felt such motivation from anyone before. They lit off sparks; she had called to mind, both mentally and physically. He wasted no time and asked her to go steady and she didn't hesitate, she said yes. Their chemistry was electric; every look from him was a passionate one and every touch, just as stimulating. Studying in her bedroom and breaking off to kiss each other on top of her bed, always holding hands, fondling each other everywhere, walking her to her class, making out at her locker, taking her out to lunch, driving her down to the coast, going to the beach, kissing, petting and getting each other hot, hot and **hot**. Eduardo would always ask her to take off her bra and the one and only time she had obliged him, she felt as if she could have given her virginity away. She nearly did, his lips and tongue alone on her bare breasts felt **too** good and it took every ounce of willpower she had left to push his steamy body away. God, she really, really loved him back then and she really, really wanted to have sex with him, but she had made an oath to God to remain a virgin until her wedding night.

And her wedding night wasn't so magical; in fact, Eduardo Sanchez left an embedded image that all men would be just like him and her husband was often drunk, sloppy and selfish and she had to settle for his mediocre love-making and ten years of second-rate affection until his untimely death. She had been a lonely widow for the past two years, full of false optimism and crummy one-night stands, searching for something better until today when she felt as if she just walked into the den of hope.

"How are you?"

Stacey couldn't help but beam, "Fine, how are you?"

"I'm good, great in fact."

Stacey continued to smile, "I didn't know you were an associate here."

"I didn't know they hired you; didn't put two and two together that Stacey **Somers** could be Stacey **Mitchell**."

"Yah, married right out of college, to a medical student in fact. But I'm a widow now...are you married?" She asked looking at the ring on his finger confirming that yes; indeed he had tied the knot.

"Yes."

"Happy?" Now why did she just ask that?

Eduardo hesitated. His heart was pounding uncontrollably. Stacey was beginning to affect him the way Amber used to—he had to get it under control. He was **so** happy to see her and couldn't understand why, "Very happy."

"Too bad," Stacey replied.

**Too bad?** Good God, he was in definite trouble. Knowing women as well as he did, he knew at once that Stacey Mitchell wanted him; unreal. All those years ago, she could have had him, now she's lonely and opened herself up for accessibility when he's no longer obtainable? "So I see from your resume you graduated from Yale," he affirmed, changing the subject.

"I heard you graduated from Harvard?" Stacey flirted back, giving him a gamine smile.

Eduardo straightened up in his chair. Her sapphire eyes entranced him. "Harvard-Yale, the great rivalry," he quipped, crossing his arms across his chest.

Stacey let go a cute little laugh then flipped back her blond hair away from her shoulders. "We're not going to break out in a boxing match now are we?"

And Eduardo watched her attentively as she tossed back those blond locks. Tossing hair to one's side indicated to him that a female was interested in him. Eduardo knew now that he was in so much trouble. He liked the cat and mouse game; and missed it just as much. "That all depends," he let go, his voice deepening with every syllable.

"On what?" She asked in her own seductive timbre.

Eduardo's sexuality overwhelmed him all at once, "On you yielding."

Stacey's mouth dropped open wide as she gazed away, pretending to look somewhere else. Blushing profusely, she tried to calm herself down. How does he do that? His overpowering magnetism pulled her in, inch by every satisfying inch, simply conversing with him, she wanted to throw herself onto his desk and kiss that sensuous mouth of his. "Us Yale grads never surrender," Stacey presented, calm as ever, "Especially to Harvard grads."

"Good," Eduardo asserted, back to business. "Because Aldridge & Watson needs a first-class contract's associate and by the rest of your resume, I see you have nothing but agreement experience."

Stacey couldn't stop staring at him, Eduardo seemed unresponsive to her usual glamour. His wife must be some looker to have him bound so tight. But then she realized something else, as she allowed him more of a view of her silky thighs by crossing her legs; **oh yes**, Eduardo was still a healthy man. Stacey couldn't help but notice Eduardo as he brought his eyes down to her legs to take a peek at her shapely limbs. **Oh hell yes**, Eduardo Sanchez was still a red-blooded vigorous male who was used to getting what he desired; anything that he **so** desired.

Although he tried, it didn't matter. Philip Aldridge threw Stacey and Eduardo together every chance he got. Eduardo was working on a settlement agreement, Stacey was asked to join. Eduardo had a mediation conference; Stacey was asked to sit in. Wherever he went, she was suddenly there. Enticing him, reminding him of the times she used to fend his body off. Those terrible teenage years—when he gave her eleven months of his full attention; dates on the beach, movies and dinners, dancing, alone with her in the back seat of his car. Making out, rolling around on the leather interior until blisters would appear from the friction against his pants. So near to bringing Stacey to surrender but she **still** would manage to push his fervent body away.

Was he simply curious? He certainly wasn't interested. But why was Stacey rapidly consuming all of his thoughts? Was it the chase? The thrill of the hunt? She made him turn his head that was it. He was stone when it came to work; he was focused, engrossed—now he was nothing short of sidetracked! Stacey was his equal in intelligence and he suddenly found himself admiring her. She was not only stunning, she was self-assured and exuded confidence and he hadn't been this engrossed since...he had to keep reminding himself that there was once a woman who distracted him to **tears**. Good God, how he loved that woman! His son's mother...Amber.

"Are you free for lunch?"

Eduardo looked up from his reading. "No, I've got to head downtown in a few minutes, I have a meeting."

Stacey stood firm in the doorway. "Can you drop me off at the corner of Robertson and Melrose then?"

Eduardo gazed into her eyes. Why? How the hell was she going to get back? He sure wasn't going to offer to pick her up if that's what she was hinting at, "What's at Robertson and Melrose?"

Stacey grinned and stepped into his office and subsequently closed the door halfway. "Oh, that's just an excuse really. I'd like to talk with you in private."

Eduardo tapped his pen on his desk and contemplated his next move. He was suddenly startled by Jackie, his Legal Assistant trying to make her way in side to side the half-closed doorway, but Stacey was practically hoarding the darn entrance as Jackie tried to squeeze her way through.

"Eduardo, I need you look at something before you go," Jackie suddenly spurted out, gazing at either one of them.

"I'll meet you outside Stace," he said looking at Jackie now. "What do you need Jackie?"

Stace? Jackie thought; they're on a first name basis now?


Later, Eduardo and Stacey were in the back of his limousine, on their way downtown. Fifteen minutes was really all it took to get from Century City to Beverly Hills so Stacey better spit out what she had to say or forever hold her peace.

Stacey cleared her throat followed by fidgeting with her briefcase in her hand. Eduardo ran his eyes up and down her body, she was nervous, Good God, what the hell was she gonna say?

"Eduardo," Stacey barely got out, her throat closing up, "when we were younger...did you ever care about me?"

Eduardo gazed away and out his window. **Shit**. This was not what he expected to hear! He didn't want to rehash old memories. He had to focus on the task at hand; he had to go to a hearing for Yazmine's case, "Of course Stacey, why?"

"Because when I look at you, I still see...**my future**. We have so much in common, we seem to complement one another and we still have incredible chemistry."

Eduardo cleared his throat then shifted his weight around in the limousine seat. "I'm unavailable Stacey. I love my wife."

"I'm sure you do. I'm not asking you to leave her," Stacey voiced, grabbing her suitcase with all her might. "I just want to be with you...at least once."

**Oh shit!** He was really in trouble, and Good God, he hated those words "leave her" in any form that was uttered and by anyone. Eduardo looked around him and out the window again. They were almost near her drop-off point. He couldn't believe he was really contemplating this. "I'm married to the fullest extent of the word Stace...and I will never be unfaithful to her," he finally said, hoping she'd take the outlet.

Stacey swallowed her pride and stiffened up from the limo suddenly coming to a brief halt. She waited for the door to open and confessed, "Whether you realize it now or realize it later, you and I **will** become lovers."

Stacey then whisks out and shut the door behind her. Eduardo at that time looked up and across at her behind the safe tinted privacy windows of the limousine. Closing his eyes in torment, his commanding prurient nature engulfed him all at once. In the back of his mind, he knew she could be right.

# CHAPTER NINE

Amber strapped Peyton into a car seat and drove up Pacific Coast Highway on their way toward Malibu. Amber had a surprise for her son and hopefully, Peyton would grow up knowing the love and companionship Amber once shared as a child.

All her life, she's had a pet of some kind. That unconditional love and attention you could only receive from a cat or a dog. When she was ten, she had a Cockapoo named 'Candy', when she was twelve, a cat named 'Missy' and when she was in high school; she owned a Cocker Spaniel named 'Ciara'.

Amber's longtime friend had a litter of Golden Retriever puppies and Amber decided (without her husband's knowledge) that she would get their son a puppy.

They reach Malibu within twenty-five minutes and Peyton instantly wanted to know where he was. "Where are we mommy?"

"I have a surprise for you," Amber said excitedly.

"A surprise," he asked, his eyes popping out.

"Yep, and I think you're gonna like it."

Amber took Peyton out of his car seat and dropped him on the ground. She then grabbed his little hand and guided him over to the door.

Madge Humphreys greeted them at the entry and Amber gave her former neighbor a quick fond hug.

"I'm so glad to see you, gosh I've missed you," Madge gushed, kneeling down to Peyton's level, "and how are you Master Sanchez?"

Peyton turned a little shy and hid behind his mother's legs. "I'm fine, thank you."

Madge raised an eyebrow, "My-my, such big words for a little man."

"His father," Amber gibed, looking her friend up and down. Madge Humphreys used to be Amber's neighbor years ago when she was still married to Victor in Granada Hills. Amber would oftentimes gossip with Madge for hours about the other neighbors on the block, various celebrities and the week's current events. She liked Madge simply because she was so straightforward, held nothing back, told the truth always and was so darn proud of it. A straight shooter, Amber used to call her.

Amber walked in with Peyton and eyed all the luxurious furniture and the enormous glass windows that paraded a beautiful view of the ocean and beachfront property beyond.

Madge pinched her friend's arm and caused Amber to shut her wide-open mouth. "We've moved up in the world now, haven't we?"

Amber then looked into her friend's blue eyes; dirty blond hair styled high on top of her head. She was almost as tall as Amber too, nearly five ten. "I've been meaning to ask you over, when are you free for dinner?"

"Come to the Palisades? What an honor," Madge relayed, holding her hand up to her heart.

"Stop it," Amber guffawed, "I mean really, we want you over."

"How are **we** doing?" Madge stated, leading the twosome over to the living room to get a better look at the waves pounding against the surf.

Peyton climbed on top of the couch and rested his little arms over the arch overlooking the water beyond.

Amber ran her fingers through his soft black hair as she sat next to him. "We are doing fine, great in fact, I've never been happier in my entire life Madge, I'm so in love."

Madge choked back her tears and could instantly feel Amber's genuine tranquility. She cried like a baby when she heard that Amber tried to commit suicide a couple of years back. Amber was a good friend, and Madge wished to God that Amber trusted her enough to confide in her about her affair. After Madge's ugly divorce, she moved away from the neighborhood and thought she'd never see or hear from Amber again. Until last week, Madge was so overwhelmed from hearing her voice, years of friendship passed before her very eyes. "So he's good to you?"

Amber sighed, "Oh yes Madge, he's wonderful."

Madge grabbed Amber's left hand and held it within hers. She didn't want to look, but curiosity got the best of her. She then overturned her arm and there it was; the three-inch scar that Amber produced. A tear fell out of her eye. "Why didn't you contact me? I thought we were so close you and I."

Amber rubbed Madge's hand within hers. "It was spontaneous," she managed to affirm. "It wasn't planned."

Madge smiled, "It usually isn't."

Amber bit down on her lower lip.

Madge then eyed Peyton casually watching the seagulls swooping down to collect fish out of the ocean, "And this little miracle?"

"He's my blessing," Amber gushed happily, running her hand across his head of hair again. "He's gonna be four soon and mommy wanted to give him an early birthday present."

"Oh yes," Madge added, "Where are those birthday presents?"

The two women then stood up together, but Madge instantly grabbed Amber again to give her friend a meaningful hug. She whispered into her ear, "I love you Amber, I'm so happy for you that everything worked out." She then caressed her cheek and looked back at Peyton who was anxiously waiting his early birthday present. "Let's go outside, shall we?"

Amber picked up her son and set him high on her hip as she walked down the exterior toward a pen and instantly, Amber could feel Peyton's little body jump for delight upon her waist.

"Mommy—puppies!"

Amber eyed Madge while her friend went to the chain-link fence to let out the ten little bouncy, friendly, chewy, pouncing collections of beige fluff. They all run out toward Peyton instantly as he dove into receive them. He giggled, he twisted, he grabbed—he tried to pet them all—his arms were full of fur and Peyton was in puppy paradise.

"Do you like them Peyton?"

Peyton was sniggering continuously and bent down to give a couple of puppies a kiss. "Oh yes mommy, I like them."

"Which one do you want?"

Peyton froze. His eyes grew wide as saucers, "Which one? I can have one mommy? We can tak'em home with us?"

Amber sat herself on the grass and straight away three puppies dashed into her lap. A big huge smile surfaced as she leaned over to pet two puppies with both hands. "Just one; whichever one you want baby, he's your birthday present."

Peyton ran around the area and the puppies all followed him; he stopped, they stopped, he ran, they ran. He was having piles of fun. "I want that one," he pointed toward the corner.

Amber jerked her head around and lo and behold, a lone puppy was sitting in the corner watching all the other puppies joyfully wander about.  He was quiet and still, hadn't moved, but started to wag his tail the moment Peyton walked toward him.

Peyton plopped himself on the ground and offered the puppy his open arms.  The puppy hesitated, and then gradually strolled toward his new owner.  Peyton scooped the puppy up in his confine and walked him over to his mother.  "He's going to be my patient."

"Patient?" Madge asked bewildered, gazing at Amber's shocked stare.

"He wants to be a doctor when he grows up," Amber exclaimed.

"Good to know," Madge pinpointed.


Later, Amber, the new puppy, Mrs. Lopez and Peyton were all upstairs playing pretend 'Urgent Care'.  Peyton was walking around with a fake chart in his hands while Amber heard Eduardo's entrance downstairs.  She sprung to her feet and halted the fake hospital with her hands.  "Wait here, don't anyone move, I want to break it to him gently."

Mrs. Lopez shook her head, "Mr. Sanchez said **no dogs**.  I told you he's not going to like it."

Amber snorted, "Too bad, the puppy stays."

Amber then sprinted out the doorway and down the long staircase to find Eduardo wandering about searching for her.  When Eduardo sees her, his arms go wide and Amber ran into them.  They embrace long and hard when Eduardo buried his nose into her shoulder.

He began to kiss her neck but Amber backed away.  "Now don't get mad," she cautiously voiced.

"What did you do?" He asked playfully.

"Oh please don't get mad—promise me you won't get mad?" Amber begged now, her hands flat together in prayer.

Eduardo took off his suit jacket and laid it down on the foyer chair. He was feeling nothing but guiltiness lately, spending too much time at work thinking about that blond; her legs, her allure, the way she walked around confident and smiling during the day. "OK—really, what did you do?"

Amber could tell his voice was stern, but there was also something else in his face she just couldn't place her finger on. Amber let her intuition roll off her shoulders; she was just too revved up to pursue his mystified expression. "OK...oh hell, just come with me upstairs." Amber subsequently grabbed his arm and led him up the staircase.

Eduardo headed toward their bedroom, thinking that they were about to make love, but then Amber detoured them into the opposite direction toward their son's room.

Eduardo walked in surprised to see Mrs. Lopez lying on the floor, while Peyton pretended to operate on her.

Peyton's eyes lit up within seeing his daddy and ran to him instantly, "Daddy—Daddy! Look at my patients! Look at my patients!"

"I know, I know I see her," he laughed, scooping his little boy into his arms and hugging his body near. Then, without warning, he noticed the ball of fluff sitting on the right near Peyton's bed. The puppy started to wag his tail, but remained seated; his little legs bent and twisted sideways, tissue paper wrapped around one paw. Eduardo turned toward his wife and Amber smirked, then beamed, shut her eyes and was about to burst with glee.

"Oh baby, he loves him. They're kindred spirits those two. You should see how he follows Peyton around, it's **so** adorable—it's as if he's been here forever."

Eduardo bent down and placed Peyton back onto the ground. Peyton hurriedly stomped toward his new puppy and gave him a huge hug. Peyton then began to wrap tissue paper around the puppy's other paw.

Eduardo was in disbelief, but his heart sunk at the sight of his little boy deliriously happy. Amber noted her husband's acceptance and threw herself into his arms. Eduardo wrapped his hands around her back and hugged her near.

"Guess what his name is?" She whispered into his ear.

"What?" Eduardo quietly mouthed.

"Patience."

Eduardo laughed, twirled his wife around then picked her up within his arms and headed toward their bedroom.

Mrs. Lopez just rolled her eyes on the ground from their sudden burst of ardor.

# CHAPTER TEN

Amber hated when Eduardo was sent out of town to work on a case. Even though he was gone for only a couple a day's at a time, it felt like an eternity when he wasn't warming her bed.

Amber went to their closet and smelled his suits hanging on the far end. Oh Lord, she loved his scent. Musk, cologne, oranges—sex comes to mind. The whiff intoxicated her and instantly ignited her sexual urge. She took his grey blazer off the rack and walked into the bedroom to lay the suit on top of other clothes she had already laid out on the mattress for him.

With a fervent smile embraced to her face, Amber began to disrobe and strolled toward the bathroom where Eduardo was taking his shower. He hadn't noticed her approach, having to rinse out the shampoo out of his hair and Amber quietly closed the door behind her and watched her husband as he casually washed out the soap. **He's still magnificent**, Amber thought happily. Turning forty-one that year, Eduardo nevertheless had the body of a twenty-five year-old male. The ideal male physique, broad shoulders, tall frame, muscular tone legs...his awesome package.

Amber brought her eyes up from her husband's luster to find Eduardo curious with a boyish grin.

"What do you think you're doing?"

Amber smiled and grabbed the soap. "I'm giving you a proper send-off, now turn around, I want to wash your back."

Eduardo did what he was told, and laid his hands flat on the ceramic tiles behind him. Amber next took the soap and rubbed it all around his shoulders and lower extremities. Eduardo directly became stiff from the smooth, silky contact. Amber heard Eduardo groan and she could no longer restrain herself from wanting that body of his plunging inside her. Amber dropped the soap and bent down and appeared suddenly in between his spread out arms on the other side. Eduardo immediately kissed his wife as she wrapped her arms around his neck and entangled her body into his.

Jackie was sitting opposite Eduardo taking dictation. Suddenly, the door opened and Stacey popped her head through. "Have a moment?"

"I'll be right back," Jackie said standing up.

"No Jackie, sit back down, what do you need Stace?"

He called her 'Stace' again; Jackie thought suspiciously, a shortened name for Stacey. Gee, so intimate with the new associate in such a short time. What the heck was going on?

"Dr. Watson wanted me to go over these figures with you later, when you have a chance?" Stacey asked quickly.

"Why didn't you just have your secretary give them to me?"

"I don't have one yet," Stacey said quickly.

"Oh, I'll mention it to Martin. You can borrow mine until they hire one for you."

Jackie threw a scowl at Eduardo. Eduardo ignored Jackie's hardened look.

"That sounds good, I'll be back later," Stacey uttered, turning around and heading toward the door.

Jackie was still fuming and watched Eduardo as he probed Stacey's derriere as she exited out of his office.

Eduardo turned immediately toward Jackie. Jackie's rage subsided as her posture softened.

"What?"

"What?" She asked back.

"Let's get back to work," he said, taking control of an out of control situation.

Jackie decided right then and there that maybe tomorrow was a good time to go and visit Amber.

They hug and wipe tears away from seeing each other again. Amber had always been jealous of Jackie Medina, she had been Eduardo's assistant for the past ten years; but seeing her today, brought forth agonizing memories of a past that she wanted to forget.

"I knew he was in love with you," Jackie voiced, sort of matter-of-factly.

"How?" Amber wondered.

"One day, while we were in the conference room, we were watching a Power Point and the curtains were drawn. You know those silly curtains that you can see out from the inside, but are not able to see from the outside in?

"Oh yah, I remember those, then what?"

"Well, it was dark, and I sat directly behind Eduardo, sort of on the side of him on his left and we were both concentrating on the Power Point when I saw in the corner of my eye his head turning. I gazed at him while his head completely turned and I noticed that he was looking at someone beyond the curtain. He was looking at **you**! You had walked past the curtain, probably didn't know we were on the inside and sat down at the empty desk directly across from him. You started to type at the computer and then all of a sudden, you turned toward him and buried your face within your hands. I noted Eduardo's reaction because he seemed to straighten up in his chair. He looked up once more at the Power Point and then turned back instantly to look at you again. You had your face inside your hands still and then covered your forehead with just one hand. You looked lost and sad, I wondered what you were thinking and Eduardo couldn't take his eyes off of you! I couldn't believe it, his shoulders began to slump...it was as if he knew what you were thinking."

"Oh my God," Amber uttered, "I remember that day, I was thinking about him! He was driving me crazy, I couldn't concentrate on my work, I wanted to be with him, and I didn't know how."

"Oh Amber, that's so romantic. However it began, I truly believe that you two were meant to be together, I truly do."

Amber hugged her former co-worker near, "Now you didn't come all the way over here to tell me **that** did you?"

"No—I, gosh, I've missed you Amber, would you ever go back to the office?"

"No, Eduardo doesn't want me to work—ever. Says I don't need to. Now, you're changing the subject."

"That's really too bad, we miss you there."

"Why?"

Jackie found a seat on a nearby couch, even though she considered Amber a friend; they never had a chance to become really close. "Amber, you know I've always been up front with you. I understand why you felt you needed to keep your affair with Eduardo quiet. The gossip at Aldridge & Watson runs rampant sometimes. Some people just can't keep their mouths shut."

Alarm bells went off in Amber's head. "Why? What have you heard?"

Jackie admired Amber's natural beauty, "I consider you a friend and I need to let you know something."

"What?" Amber asked on pins and needles.

"There's a new attorney in the office."

Then Amber's heart suddenly dropped, "What's her name?"

"Stacey Somers. She's this petite, voluptuous little blond who has a chip on her shoulder. She's authoritative and bossy and seems to have some kind of past connection with Eduardo."

At that very moment, all of Amber's security flew right out the window. Eduardo loved her—loved her enough to take care of her and Peyton; he loved her, he loved her and **he loves her**...why was he suddenly attracted to this Stacey Somers? Amber felt nervous all of sudden and her stomach began to ache. Good Lord, she knew this couldn't be true. Why would her husband lie? Eduardo said he would never abandon her—**ever**.

"Amber, you OK? I'm sorry; maybe I shouldn't have mentioned it to you."

"No Jackie, you did the right thing. I love you, thank you for letting me know."

"You sure?"

"Absolutely."


Two weeks later, Amber decided to see for herself who this Stacey Somers was. Amber was Eduardo's **wife**, and she had every right on Earth to make sure her husband wasn't foolin' around. She made several calls to Jackie during the week to form a bridge of communication between wife and assistant. The assistant would give the heads up to the wife and notify her if anything was awry. Jackie called Amber around ten o'clock that morning to let her know that Eduardo and Stacey were planning to go out to lunch that afternoon. Lunch?

**How dare him**, Amber seethed. How dare he have lunch with another woman! Damn, or does she allow this behavior? Does she trust him? She used to. But she knew, deep down inside her soul, Amber knew something just didn't feel quite right. Eduardo and this Stacey Somers; their friendship, their proper acquaintance, their former association, their close profession—screamed misrepresentation.

As soon as she hung up the phone with Jackie, Amber ran to the shower and began her long process of bringing her husband to his knees.


Amber was on her way up to the twenty-fifth floor of the Avenue of the Stars building, the suite that housed Aldridge & Watson. She was inside an elevator and began to admire herself in the shiny golden reflection staring back at her. She smiled, because she knew she looked **amazing**. Summer was in full bloom and it was hot and humid outside. Amber enjoyed a full length tan from sunning herself outside by her pool daily. She had been a Golden Goddess; her long black hair freed and draped alongside her shapely shoulders. The excellence of her white linen halter dress enhanced her impeccable breasts. Her legs, tone and smooth, not a flaw or nick from the razor from shaving her legs in a huff. White spaghetti strapped Jimmy Choo's, at least an inch high, something she never wore because of her self-consciousness about her five foot eleven frame. But she was on a mission; the destruction of Stacey Somers, ammunition enough to blow her petite little ass outta the water.

Amber calmly opened up the suite to the reception area. So many memories dashed inside her head. She had forgotten she had not stepped into the place since the night of the suicide attempt. Bittersweet memories surfaced immediately, times when she wasn't able to touch him, only allowed to chat with him in the office or in the hallways and only then for a few short moments.

Amber went straight through the entrance door without formerly announcing herself and headed straight toward her husband's office. She eyed Jackie first and was just about to ask her where Eduardo was when a familiar voice broke through her concentration.

"There is a God and he loves me."

Amber didn't bother to turn around...Awe, Gordon Daggert, still the same cocky bull. Amber slowly twisted around and caught Gordon's wonder. Still the dusty blond hair but shaved his mustache since the last time she'd see him, piercing baby-blue's. He looked...**charming** for some reason...cuter than she used to think. Then again, she only had eyes for one man. "Unbelievable you haven't been arrested."

Gordon laughed, "Me? Why? What for?"

"Sexual harassment," Amber let go wickedly.

Gordon chuckled at the notion, "Key there is to always leave them satisfied."

Amber rolled her eyes and smiled. Gordon always reminded her of her husband and his smug attitude. "You keep telling yourself that, Sparky."

Gordon sure did miss Amber, she was one girl who could always give as good as she got. "You still look stunning," Gordon stood amazed and brought his eyes up and down Amber's tall gorgeous frame. "I thought for a moment that I'd have to propose, **Mrs. Sanchez.**"

Amber beamed and eyed Jackie—who, by the way had a crush on Gordon for as long as she could remember—come alive in the corner of her eye. "Why thank you sir."

"No—I mean you look absolutely astounding."

"Again, I thank you," Amber replied, winking at Jackie behind Gordon.

Gordon turned to look at whom Amber was grinning at. The two ladies exchanged mischievous glares, "What are you girls up to? Can I come along?" Gordon asked, wanting every part of Amber against his mouth.

The two woman laugh, how'd he know? "His door was closed; you didn't tell him did you?" Amber asked Jackie, who was now nodding her head.

"Oh—no, they left about fifteen minutes ago," Jackie said, standing directly beside Gordon now.

Gordon gazed down at Jackie looking up at him. "You two are up to no good, aren't you?" He smiled, presenting Jackie with an ardent grin.

Jackie blushed, "Can you tell?"

Gordon gazed over at Amber again. "Oh yah—Amber is dressed to kill," he said, eating her with his eyes again. "So where do you ladies want to eat? My treat," he let go, holding out his elbows for them to put their hands through; the semi-gentleman he thought he was.

Amber thought about it for a moment. She wanted to catch her husband in the act of something, but that something was still just a presumption, and now, Gordon wanted to come along? Did he already know something? But what did he know? Gordon better come along, she would need his good looks and attraction in her corner if...**Good Lord**, if her husband was truly cheating on her!

"The Four Seasons," Jackie quietly voiced.

"A hotel," Amber questioned in disbelief.

Jackie lowered her eyes, "Yes."

**The fuckin' Four Seasons?** Amber thought, incredulous.

Gordon noted the impassioned look on Amber's face. This was turning out to be a helluva day!

As soon as they all sat down, Amber eyed all the patrons and there was no sight of her husband and some blond. "Are you sure they're here?" A displeasing sinking feeling entered her heart. Were they already upstairs in a room?

"There he is," Jackie said hushing her voice down, pointing in an easterly direction.

Amber turned her head around. **He sure was...**Eduardo and some blond. Her flaxen hair pulled back into a power pony-tail, ideal for the smart woman on the go. She was pretty too, a lovely little thing and come to think of it, she was kinda Playboy-hot with a sultry look—blond with a brain—his former 'unique' type. **Goddamn him!** But she still had to give her husband the benefit of the doubt. What if they were just discussing work? Going over case studies...their point of attack on a case they were working on?

Gordon noted Amber's curious expression. "Stacey Somers, have you met her yet?"

"No," she quickly relayed, turning her head back around.

Gordon laughed under his breath. "She's a bitch."

Amber turned to look in to Gordon's blue eyes, "Really?"

"Oh—yah, she's hell on wheels. I tried to hit on her the first week she was here but she doused my fire real quick. She's unattainable."

**Unattainable**...Amber thought, rolling her eyes. She knew that word all too well. Oh hell, Amber was really livid now! Eduardo loved that challenge. His commanding prurient nature was probably swelling him to mass proportions as they spoke. Amber clinched her linen napkin and began to practically rip it apart.

Gordon looked across at Eduardo with Stacey and then quickly back at Amber and her visible lack of confidence. He immediately came up with a plan and decided to come to her rescue and spilled a glass of water onto Jackie's lap causing an overreacting woman to spring up from her seat and make a spectacle of herself. It worked. Faces all around them began to look toward the hubbub.

Amber remained calm and didn't look his way. If Eduardo was going to look in the direction of the turmoil, then Amber was definitely **not** going to make it appear that she was spying on him...Even though she was.

When her heart began to pound out of control, Amber knew that her husband had been approaching. She could always tell when he was around or in close proximity.

"What's going on?"

Amber casually gazed up at him. The blond was nowhere in sight. How convenient. "Well hello there, aren't you going to say hello to your wife?"

Eduardo appeared confused. A deer caught in the headlights; stiff and unresponsive. "I would when she tells me what she's doing here," he voiced, giving a quick look over at Jackie. Jackie gazed away and rolled her eyes then crossed her arms.

"I came by and met Jackie for lunch. Gordon's just trimming."

Gordon laughed and then his amusement was diminished by Eduardo's cold hard stare. **Asshole**, serves him right for spending so much time with that blanched siren.

"Can I speak with you alone?"

Gordon stood up and grabbed Jackie's hand. "Com'on sweetie, the lovebirds need a moment."

Jackie walked away with him and her heart thumped with glee.

"I was in the middle of lunch Eduardo...Oh; by the way, what are **you** doing here? I didn't know you practiced eating alone," Amber offered, looking around him and toward his empty table and seat. "You should have called me; I could have met you here as well." Just then, Amber stood up and made sure her husband got an eyeful of her glamorous attire.

He did all right. Eduardo brought his eyes down to her shoes then suddenly elevated up to her hazel mockery. Eduardo duly noted his wife dripped in jewels; his presents of romance on her wrists, fingers, draped all around her neck and hanging down from her ears. Every single Harry Winston bauble he ever bought her. What the hell was the special occasion?

Before he even opened his mouth, Amber blurted, "They're for armor," she jested, adjusting her five-carat diamond solitaire on her wedding finger first then dangling her diamond tennis bracelet around her wrist, "Nothing like coming to Beverly Hills without showing off how big my husband's dick is."

Boy, she knew him too well. And then suddenly, his heart dropped. Amber was dressed to impress **on purpose**. To what design, and for what intent? What does she **think** she knows and determined to find out? Good God, he'd better get his libido under control!

Amber studied his facial expression for a moment. The downward curvature of his lower lip gave him away. He was caught. But in what, she didn't quite know just yet. Was it the beginning of a temptation? She could almost bet on it. "Don't play me for a fool husband, I know you like the back of my hand. Now, I'm going to give you a kiss and send you back to work—and that's **work** little boy. Keep your zipper up and everything will be just fine. I'll see you at home."

Amber purposely flipped her hair away from her bronzed shoulders and walked away and noted all the curious Beverly Hills gossip mongrels and made sure every one of them caught an eyeful of her glorious departure.

Eduardo's emotions were turmoil. His wife left in a skilled moment. Good God, Amber looked every bit of phenomenal. What was the Goddamn fascination with

Stacey anyhow?  Was it because he's never bedded her before and he was still so curious on what that felt like?  But he knew what it felt like to bed women he's desired before, what was so Goddamn special about Stacey?  All sexual urges toward other women were supposed to cease and desist once you were married to the woman of your dreams.  Or was he simply human after all?  Amber was his **true love**, the woman he's always wanted and would practically die for—**did die for**, rolled over, made a fool of himself over—why was he so Goddamn interested in Stacey Somers anyhow?

# CHAPTER ELEVEN

Eduardo was sent out of town again; only this time the big boss insisted on Stacey going along as well to help with the contracts. On the case in Sacramento, they stayed at the five-star luxury Hyatt Regency hotel directly across from the state capitol, but their rooms were stationed down the hall from each other; temptation, only fifteen feet away.

"How about a nightcap?"

"No, I'm going to go over some notes I made today while in court."

"Oh com'on, you can do those tomorrow, you look tense, you look like you could use a drink."

Stacey waited exactly thirty minutes before she walked down the corridor thirty steps towards his room. She knew he had been inside. She had left him only thirty minutes prior right after being dropped off by their town car. Thirty minutes was really all it was going to take to spin her plan into motion...thirty minutes was all it was going to take to get Eduardo Sanchez into bed. If he were interested, he would take the temptation. If he were **still** interested...

All during the negotiations she had studied his eyes, inspected his speech and scoped out his body movement for any tell tale signs of being still engrossed. Had she been reading all his interest wrong? Whenever he looked at her, his eyes would always gaze down at her lips; did that mean he wanted to kiss her? She would oftentimes catch him checking out her bottom while she walked away; did that mean he was trying to imagine what it was like to be in bed with her? Was she reading too much into it? Was his curiosity just past tense or in the present?

Stacey's blue eyes widened and pulled Eduardo's chain. He was captivated by her allure again and his salacious nature peeked. "One drink wench," he teased, taking off his coat first as he walked across to her room.

Stacey walked over to the bar. Two wineglasses had already been conveniently set out with a bottle of open wine and Eduardo took note of them.

"Expecting company?" He asked, watching her pour white zinfandel into a glass.

She grinned, "You, of course."

"What makes you so sure of yourself?" He asked huskily.

"Because the last few months have been torture for both of us," Stacey decidedly said.

"Maybe for you," Eduardo spat out, grinning.

Stacey swallowed the fun and continued, "...And knowing you as well as I do, you wouldn't pass up this chance of being with me."

"So certain, I see," he said, lowering his eyes to her bosom by mistake.

Stacey watched him intently as he did so, "Just determining the facts sir and as I read them...you can't wait to kiss me."

Eduardo gulped. It was true, he wanted to. But Good God, he loved Amber so. He stood his ground a few steps away from her however, fighting the urge to grab her into his arms and kiss the hell out of her lips and continued to debate it. He's had women before throw themselves at him, remaining calm was easy for him. It was like riding a bike and he rather enjoyed toying with her affections. He rather liked having the tables being turned. "It can wait," he confessed, reaching over to the table and grabbing his glass of zinfandel. The irony quenched his thirst like a jug of Gatorade.

Stacey watched him keenly, and maybe just a little bit discouraged as Eduardo sipped his wine. What else could she try? She was already wearing next to nothing! Should she just jump on him? Strip for him? Unzip his zipper and start to play with it? Good heavens, she never did those things to her husband...why did she feel so naughty when around Eduardo? She required him intoxicated, maybe that would work. A little alcohol to mix up one's judgment was always a no brainer and used one too many times as a recognized excuse for adultery and her own pretext for recent sexual encounters. She had to keep him inside her room a little while longer or at least long enough for a second glass of wine. "You were brilliant, by the way."

Eduardo turned to look at her first before walking away to peek out of the window, "In what way?"

Stacy poured herself another glass of wine, "In the way you handled the settlement negotiations," she said, pausing to take a sip; then to lower down her glass, "I would have never thought to reduce my percentage rate to seize any deal. One's perception is to always offer higher to make one's goal." Stacey stood her ground directly across from him; her feet spread apart in a flirty sort of stance as she prepared herself for nearly anything and started with feeding his ego. Stacey did think of his same angle early on but opted to stay null to watch her colleague spin his magic so that she could possibly secure a green light for her true objective—which was to get him into bed.

Eduardo smiled to himself, that was his original plan but then came up with another when the opposing attorney let it slip that his client had been hurting for money.  Offering a lower amount had always been Plan B.  "This negotiation could have been handled via e-mail or over the phone if you ask me," he suddenly said, acting as if he were about to leave.  But he then continued to sip his wine and gazed out at the view of the lights surrounding the capitol building through the hotel window.

"A face-to-face negotiation and coming to Sacramento was a good idea Eduardo, there really is no need to second guess our plan when it's worked out so well."  Stacey noticed his glass was nearly empty and walked over by his side to retrieve it.

Eduardo's head whipped around within seeing her arrival next to him and offered her his empty glass.

Stacey carefully poured him another drink then seductively stepped away; could feel his eyes undress her from behind...also in her plan.  But then she became disappointed when she realized he hadn't been looking.  She noticed his reflection in the mirror as she passed it by that he had swiftly turned his head away.  Why was he so difficult to read!  "What are you afraid of?" She asked, trying another route.

Eduardo lowered his glass, "Afraid?  Who's afraid?"

"You are," she voiced softly, sipping her own glass of wine.  "You can have me now...she won't know."

Stacey brought 'she' into the picture and three was definitely a crowd.  Unbeknown to the blond, the brunette just came back to him in full force.  "I will know," he said, walking away from one window to go and take a lookout another for no good reason.

Eduardo pulled back the curtains that hid the gorgeous nighttime view and then quickly turned around to find Stacey disrobed.  Now...why did she have to go and do something as motivating as that?

"What does a girl have to do..." she asked, fingering her bare cleavage seductively, "to get you to go to bed with her?"

Eduardo lowered his glass and then gently placed it on a nearby coffee table. She was marvelous...he hadn't seen another woman naked in a really long time. She was also in perfect shape for her age, her breasts were still plump and her nipples rose to the occasion, they were a little on the medium side—compared to his wife's—but they were nice to look at, and maybe, as his mouth grew watery, nice to tongue as well. Her stomach was tone and flat and she was wearing lace panties with garter belts and silk stockings, a sure-fire cock-snare and felt his manhood swell with the bait. He closed his eyes. It was an opportunity of a lifetime. How many nights had he come home sexually frustrated because Stacey had denied him of intercourse from his failed attempts back in high school? Too many to count...she had repelled him so many times in the past and now here she was, practically lying down with her legs wide open? He shook his head, "I'm flattered Stace...but I'm happily married."

Stacey watched in awe as her one-chance retreated toward the door. She redressed herself and had no rebuttal. She didn't have to; she knew exactly what was on his mind. He truly loved his wife, she realized. Oh how she wished that **she** were his wife!

Stacey would never have him though, not while Amber Sanchez was alive.

# Chapter TWELVE

Eduardo stepped off the plane and grabbed his suitcases and headed toward the limousine area. Seeing his limo parked alongside the others, the driver waved him down. Eduardo nodded the confirmation and headed toward his transportation. He maintained an incredible guilty conscience for having nearly slept with Stacey and vowed to never come that close again. If Philip wanted both of them together, then **he'd** better damn come along. Eduardo would never be that tempted to have an affair ever again.

The driver took his bags and put them in the trunk. Eduardo waited on the curb for just a moment while the attendant opened up the door for him to expose long sexy tan legs waiting for him on the inside.

Eduardo hesitated—his heart dropped—leaned in and then followed the woman's legs up to her face and then grinned from ear to ear.

Oh how she always seemed to take his breath away! Dressed in a long fur coat, high heels and nothing underneath, Amber widened the cover to unwrap her breasts to his excitable mouth.

"I missed you," she said running her hands through his hair while he continued to brush his lips across her skin.

"I missed you too," he said, feeling shamefaced.

"I love you."

"I love you too," he said grabbing her body near. He buried his head in the crux of her neck and kissed her tenderly. "Help me unbuckle my pants."

"You are so bad Mr. Sanchez," Amber teased; doing as she was told.

"You wouldn't want me any other way," he said, laying down on the car seat and drawing her body over his torso. Eduardo grabbed her waist and ran his hands gently up her smooth stomach toward her ample breasts and hardened nipples. "You're the most beautiful woman I've ever seen."

**Seen? What the hell does that mean,** Amber thought, as she began to move her hips on his erection. A part of her—that that deep down insecure part of her—felt it was a slipup on his part. **Seen?** Who had he **seen** lately? And a little-red flag rose up inside Amber's head; it was pandemonium for her woman's intuition. What other woman had he been with since her?

**Stacey Somers,** she realized, feeling herself climax immediately. She got off his waist abruptly, pulled the coat back over her nakedness and then shut her eyes.

"What's wrong?" He asked, expecting to get a passionate kiss from her like she usually did after they made love.

"Nothing, I just had a cramp in my leg, that's all." She easily gave to him lying through her teeth.


Later at home and within the next couple of days, Amber knew Eduardo had been lying a lot. Her husband became a different man all of a sudden and suddenly didn't act the same way toward her. One night, Amber did ask him point blank if he were having an affair, and he told her no, but she still didn't believe him. A little piece of her began to die as she became to realize that Eduardo Sanchez could never really be completely hers. He was still just a man…a man with a roving eye, and maybe it was karma to have the tables suddenly being turned on her.  Somewhere in her heart she had that deep down fear of being cheated on like Victor and Leticia.  It would definitely be karma, a complete circle, her unlucky fortune cookie or that dreaded repercussion.  That unknown of your spouse secretly deceiving you, the evitable happening and Amber continued to use those excuses to drink because she knew…deep down, she knew her husband was lying to her.

And Eduardo was constantly on guard.  Buried down, he never wanted to hurt her and knew that Amber would never accept his honesty even if all that happened was Stacey coming onto him but his wife continued with the pushing and the probing while he remained mysterious and avoided Amber now in anticipation of some emotional war.

They were a couple caught in a game; a game of truth or dare.

# CHAPTER **THIRTEEN**

Amber sat on the couch alone and poured herself another drink. Eduardo had not come home yet. Recently, that was all he ever did—come home late. She knew that routine, there were nights when she wouldn't get home until ten o'clock in the evening. Overextended lunches, missed calls, lie after lie until she couldn't distinguish what was the truth and what wasn't. All her life she was never that untrustworthy, all her life she was always told to tell the truth and when she was secretly seeing Eduardo behind her husband's back, she got so good at being untruthful, she would test Victor to see if he could actually catch her in a lie, but he never did. How could Victor have been so oblivious? Why did he trust her so much? What was his wife doing out so late? Did **'working overtime'** really mean working until ten o'clock at night? How stupid do you have to be? Or do you really have to be that trustworthy, or deaf, dumb and blind? In Victor's mind, Amber was faithful to him, in body and soul and she never understood that sort of trust, until now.

Amber had to give her husband the benefit of the doubt; she had to believe his words, his mysterious actions and most recently, his tardiness. The bottom line, she had to trust him. Trust him enough that he would never do that to **her**.

Amber was in love…Amber was in hell because of it and it had been three long months; Amber counted, bringing another sip to her lips, three whole months since they stopped having sex, three full months since they stopped greeting one another at the door, three long months since they've showed each other affection, three long drooling months since Eduardo started acting peculiar.  Three extra long months since (according to Jackie) Stacey Somers started working at Aldridge & Watson.

Amber heard the door finally open and Eduardo lay his keys down on the foyer china cabinet.  She heard him walk over to the side of the couch, but he still said nothing.  Amber doesn't even turn around to greet him, she knew what he was looking at—or rather judging—and let out a disgusting sigh and headed up the staircase.  Amber downed the last of the Vodka and ran up the stairs to confront him.

"Why don't you just admit it?" She yelled off the top of her lungs.

Eduardo just stared at her; he doesn't even know who she is anymore!  Amber's hair was all greasy; she hadn't bothered to take a shower and she looked like **that** for a couple of days now, wearing the same damn clothes he'd seen her in since Monday and it was now Wednesday—her face was even pale and emaciated—she looked more like a zombie than some natural beauty.  This was **not** the woman that he adored; this was just some visitor he wished would go away.  "Admit what?"

"That you're fucking her!"  Amber exclaimed, losing her balance from the room tipping over and beginning to spin.

"You're delirious Amber," he relayed, stepping away from her approach, "And I'm not going to have this conversation with you when you're drunk."

"I'm not drunk—oh you'll know when I'm drunk!"

Eduardo began to get undressed and Amber stood back and enjoyed the show. Eduardo began to take off his tie, then his shoes, unbuckled his belt and pulled down his pants. His dress shirt hung low and covered his boxers and when he began to unbutton the remaining buttons to his shirt, he stood idle before her with his shirt wide open. Exposing his incredible tight muscled chest, Amber nearly expired, he hadn't touched his wife in nearly three months and he was sure she wondered why. Before, all they had to do was just look at each other and they'd be tearing each other's clothes off. Now he couldn't look her directly in the face?

"You're fucking her, and I want you to stop lying to me," Amber quietly mouthed, sitting down in the bathroom, directly across from her husband's enticing body.

"I'm not going into this with you."

Amber's heart dropped. Good Lord so it was true? "How long have you been fucking her? Oh wait," she laughed sickly, "Let me guess, three months."

Eduardo stared at her agape, "No, that's just how long my wife has been drinking."

Amber's mouth closed, "Liar. You're fucking your new attorney and now you're lying to me!"

Eduardo drew down his boxer shorts at last and released himself of his shirt. He stood naked in front of her for a few short seconds and then grabbed a nearby towel to wrap it around his torso.

Amber started to weep; Eduardo looked at her and his penis remained flaccid. This was not the man she married. This was not the man who practically ate her when they were intimate.

Unemotional, Eduardo gazed down at her as he strode across from her into the bathing area. He went to turn on the water to the shower, turned around and then watched her in contempt as she continued to shed tears on the floor...Where the hell was his wife?  He didn't even feel sorry for her.  "I'm not the one who's broken the connection Amber, you are.  You're denying me of the woman I used to love.  I don't know who you are anymore.  I haven't cheated on you, nor would I ever.  But honest to God, if you don't stop with the excessiveness, you're going to force an outcome you won't be proud of."

Amber looked up and across at him releasing himself of his towel and stepping into the shower.  She could stop, she could, but he would have to make the first move, he had to stop lying first.  He was being deceitful and he was holding something back, she knew this, and she could feel it in her bones.

She opened up the shower door and yelled, "You're lying to me!  Don't you think I can sense it when you're lying?  I can feel it Eduardo.  Something's changed, we don't make love anymore, you come home late—and you've been looking at me with disgust in your eyes.  You told me once that you would always love me no matter what.  Well, this is no matter what Eduardo, and I can feel that you're distracted by someone else!"

Amber really didn't mean to do it, but when she went to shut the sliding glass door, she slammed it so hard, she shattered it.

"Look what you did you drunken **idiot!**  You could have killed me!" Eduardo exclaimed, grabbing a towel and stepping over the destroyed enclosure.

Amber was in shock.  He called her an 'idiot' and more tears began to fall down her face immediately.  Name-calling definitely confirmed a lack of devotion.  "Would you be honest with me please?"

"Honest about what?  I've got to take a shower in one of the guest bedrooms now."

Amber ran toward him and yanked at his arm.  "No, not until you tell me the Goddamn truth!"

"About what—I'm so fuckin mad right now Amber, I don't even want to look at you!"

Amber doesn't let go of his arm and dug her nails into his skin, "You're attracted to her, aren't you?"

He doesn't want to hurt her. He doesn't want to lie either. "Yes," he finally let go exasperated.

That was all it took. Amber fell to the floor and buried her hands between her legs and let out a terrible wail. Eduardo stood there a few more seconds, watched her in torment as she made a spectacle of herself, and went to go and take a shower in one of the spare rooms.

# CHAPTER FOURTEEN

Amber felt unloved, and when she felt unloved, she normally ran to her children.

So the following morning, Amber took off with Peyton to visit her other two children (by her first husband, Victor – yes, Eduardo's brother), Valentina and Adrian.

Victor nearly fainted within seeing his ex-wife on their front doorstep. Victor had gotten custody of both the house and their kids after filing for divorce, and had been awarded full physical custody with Amber only being awarded one hour a day under supervised visitation. She was considered 'unstable' by the court and at the time of the hearing he was overjoyed with the ruling—having felt she deserved much worse, like never seeing them again—but at present, felt the kids needed their mother and to spend some time with her. Valentina missed her mother and would often lash out at him making Victor the bad guy for having kept Amber from her. They didn't understand why, they only knew that their mother once lived in the house and then poof, she was gone.

He hadn't seen his former wife since the day of her suicide attempt and the day he last laid eyes on her lying in a hospital bed, unconscious. He was...almost relieved for a moment, shock overtaking his breath. She was still pretty, he thought, even with a silly knitted pink cap on her head in the middle of summer. He was also glad to see her to be honest. Glad to see she looked...he was going to say, **well**, but the more he stared at her the more he realized she had been crying, and something else he noticed right away too, she had been drinking. He knew from being married to her all those years that Amber only drank when she was sad. What on Earth did she have to be so unhappy about? Looking unconsciously at Peyton first, he smiled then conveyed, "What brings you to my door? You lost?"

Amber bit down on her lower lip. "Are the kids' home?" She asked, slowly shutting her eyes, trying not to cry again.

Victor shook his head and said, "No."

Amber immediately felt the coldness in his voice, "Can I wait to say hi to them? I know I'm alone and without a court-appointed guardian, but I thought I could just stop by and say hello at least."

Victor watched Peyton grab her leg and hide behind it, "The school bus will be dropping them off at the corner in about fifteen minutes—you're welcome to wait."

Amber wiped away a tear; Victor was acting like all was forgiven. She never did tell him that she was sorry. She had cut her wrist and lapsed into a coma before there was even time to offer any kind of explanation.

Amber little by little mouthed out the words 'I'm sorry' and just before she turned away, Victor stepped into her and gave her a lengthy, warm hug.

"I forgive you," he said, whispering into her ear.

She hugged him long and hard back and was so grateful for his continued friendship. She needed a friend right now. While she was in the hospital, when her mother would come to visit, she would come by with the latest news and let Amber know that Victor had gotten remarried. "How's Josie?"

Victor let go of her still smiling, "She's great, she's due in two months."

Amber stared at him agape and managed a small smile, "Really?  So you're gonna be a father again?"

Victor shoved his hands down his pockets and took another peek at Peyton, who, by this time, was hiding behind his mother's leg completely, "Yeah, we're having a girl."

Amber's heart swelled up, "That's wonderful Victor, I'm really happy for you."

"Thanks Amber," he said honestly, looking completely at Peyton now.  "And this must be..."

Amber didn't hold Peyton up this time to show him off but rather just let him linger around her leg a few more seconds.  She did however run her fingers through his head of hair.  "This is Peyton."

Victor let his smile drop; let the recognition sink in and then caught Amber's eyes beginning to swell up. "What's the matter?" He finally asked at last.

Amber stared at him again.  Should she tell him? Well, it **was** the reason why she was there in the first place! "Do you have a moment?  So we could talk?"

"Josie went to the market; she'll be back in about half an hour...is that enough time for you?"

"All I need is ten..."

Victor went to go and answer the door again.  He wasn't surprised actually to see his brother now on his front doorstep.  He still looked the same, damn him, and Victor didn't greet him with a smile, but rather a drawn out glare.

"I'm here for Amber."

"She's not here," Victor just relayed, admiring his woodwork on the door he had sand down last weekend.

"Don't play stupid with me Victor, her car's outside."

"Don't try to bully me Eduardo," Victor bit back, "Your presence doesn't frighten me.  I'm your brother, I see right through your high and mighty act. We used to wear the same K-Mart shoes you and I, or does your Harvard brain seem to forget about all that?"

Eduardo allowed the insult to roll off his hundred dollar shirt, "Where is she?" He let go exasperated.

"She's with our kids."

That hurt. He knew Victor maliciously didn't mean to say it the way, but Eduardo just felt like Victor just cut his heart out. Knowing that his brother had her first always seemed to injure his soul. "I'll wait for her."

"They went to the park, it'll probably be awhile."

Just then, a car pulled up in the driveway and Eduardo watched it come to a halt and a pregnant woman exited out of the driver's side carrying a grocery bag in her hand. She stopped short of entering, stared at Eduardo and Eduardo in turn, stared back at her. Eduardo turned to his brother, "Aren't you going to introduce us?"

Victor noted his wife's reaction to him; she was obviously entranced by his facade. Fuckin Eduardo, he wished that he'd just have an accident already and disfigure his face. "So she can fall in love with you too? Com'on Josie, just walk around him."

Josephine Sanchez walked around her brother-in-law, but her eyes never wandered off his gorgeous face.

"Whether or not you believe it Victor," Eduardo said, gazing away from his wife now entering under Victor's protective arm. "Amber **is** my soul mate, so if you want to go on believing that I stole her away from you, then you're disillusioned." He stopped abruptly when Victor crossed his arms across his chest. "Why in the hell is she here anyhow?"

"I'm her best friend," Victor quickly reported.

"Her best friend? **I'm** her best friend."

"You can't even be a husband to her."

"What is that supposed to mean?"

"She told me about the other woman Eduardo—I told you if you ever tried to hurt her or use her, I would fight to the death to protect her, and that's exactly what I'm doing."

"Is that what she told you?"

"She came over here distraught and crying—she doesn't even look the same anymore! Even **I knew** she went through a complete transformation once she tasted alcohol, why the hell didn't you? What the fuck are you doing over there Eduardo?"

Eduardo stared at Victor who suddenly got the better of him, "How convenient for you to continue to play the martyr. You don't know the truth. I told you I would never use her, she's mine and I always take care of what's mine."

Victor laughed, "Does that line really work? Cause it smells like bullshit to me."

"I don't care what you think, I love Amber."

"But you're attracted to Stacey Somers, aren't you?"

Eduardo's heart sunk. Good God, he knew? His little brother could always read him. Eduardo wanted to lie but figured what's the use. "Yes."

Victor tsked at his older brother. "Always the same womanizer—you know I've stood back and watched you in action? Envied you on how easy it was to get any woman you desired; average, sweet, incredibly gorgeous, young, older, flawless women, your entire life. And not once have I ever seen you appreciate what you had...until you slept with my wife. See, I know what you have now, there's no more begrudging **Eduardo Sanchez**...I know what it's like to hold her, to kiss her—"

Imagining his wife lying down with his little brother thoroughly undid him yet again. Eduardo cut him off right away, "Are you done yet?"

"Why, the truth hurting you Eduardo?" Victor spitefully spewed out. "I had her first **estúpido!** You don't even comprehend what you have big brother! You don't realize what you have until it's gone. **Desaparecido,** vanished."

"Shut the hell up Victor, you don't know what went on between me and her...you might think you know, but you don't."

"Have you had sex with her yet?"

"Who? Amber?"

"Stacey."

"That's none of your business."

"By you stealing my wife, you've made it my business."

Eduardo looked his little brother up and down. Couldn't believe he was still at his mercy. "I'll just wait in the car."

"Yah, you do that, run away, get the hell out."

Eduardo turned to really look at Victor. His little brother, the little pain in the ass that he always tried to hide from...the little annoying kid who was now all grown-up. Eduardo didn't know whether to keep arguing with him or give his little brother a high-five for effort. "I'm sorry Victor."

Victor bore into his brother's eyes.

"You know something Eduardo? I've come to terms with it. Oh yah, I was upset in the beginning, I even hit you in the knee with a baseball bat, recall that? That's how mad I was at you for taking her away. But later, I realized that she must have always loved you, and that's what really hurt the most. Because the more I thought about it, the more I realized that you two were always together. Sitting next to each other, walking together, laughing, swimming in the pool, she was always following you. She's never given me that much attention," he hooted, "and we were married!"

Attention?  Yah, he had that right.  Eduardo was always trying to gather up Amber's full attention, "So what advice can you give me?"

Victor looked away from him and across at Eduardo's fancy car.  "I may have been a little blind...or maybe it was just that I trusted her so much to allow her to spend so much time with you, but I remember when there was once a time the two of you were just friends.  Do you remember that?"

Eduardo did remember that.  All those years...how many were they again?  Ten—ten painstaking years of wishing and yearning to kiss Amber, hoping that she'd notice that he had been in love with her and to have her act on the attraction, "Yah, I remember."

"So she needs a friend right now."

Eduardo shoves his hands down his coat pockets.  "A friend?"

"Yes, a friend, shit, why does it have to be all or nothing with you?  If you think about big brother, this is really the hardest relationship you've ever had."

Eduardo gulped...again, he was absolutely right; school, grades, money and especially woman were effortless to him. Relationships, appreciation, empathy...those were difficult for him to always achieve. He had to get Amber to stop drinking.  Could he do it?  "Victor, do me a favor?"

Victor started to snort, "A favor?  That all depends."

"Don't tell her I was here.  I'm going home."

Victor wanted to continue talking to him really.  He missed their conversations with one another.  He missed...his **older brother**—period.  His marriage to Amber had been over years earlier even before they began having their affair.  He knew there had been something wrong in their marriage, Amber felt reserved even when he touched her back in high school and saying 'I love you' had always been so difficult for her to admit.

# CHAPTER **FIFTEEN**

It was midmorning and Amber was outside in her backyard in the hot summer sun trying to work on her tan. She was in her bikini and was rubbing tanning lotion all over her skin. Conveniently next to her was also a bottle of SKYY Vodka—quickly becoming her liquor of choice— along with a champagne glass filled with cranberry juice.

Peyton was not too far away, only about twenty yards or so kneeling in the gated sandbox his father had built for him and every now and then, he and Patience tried to do something funny that would normally put a smile on his mommy's face, but mommy continued to be sad. He tried everything to make Amber laugh, but mommy still looked gloomy.

Amber was in total anguish. If her husband was attracted to a new conquest then that meant that Amber was no longer the woman he desired. She wasn't all things to him anymore.

Peyton was laughing and playing with all his pretend patients while Amber continued to drink, her mind wandering off to a private lonely sector; a place where she could escape from today and back into the past when Eduardo once loved her and his thoughts weren't preoccupied with this new blond and she closed her eyes trying to wish it true when she popped them back open within hearing the pool man's whistling. Gazing over at him, the fella entered through the squeaky entrance pool gate. She gave him a friendly wave, and he back at her.


Dustin Jacobs, aka Dusty Denver, was an out of work adult film star, angry and preoccupied. He was thinking too much about his girlfriend who dumped him last weekend via text message and forgot the water chemistry kit he left back in the truck.

Inside the pool area and lounging already on the deck, was Mrs. Sanchez stretched out on a wrought-iron chaise longue chair, looking mighty fine, slim and put together. She looked amazing in her tight-fitting Aqua bikini over bronzed skin, so sun-kissed, so do-able and tempting. He lusted after her for a few more moments when he noticed that she was wearing a mismatched top and bottom and looked as if she were about to pass out. He's seen her like that before and shook his head from the waste and placed his net and pool pole down to go fetch the chemicals.

Meanwhile, Peyton watched the pool man wander away and out of the gate when Patience sprung to attention within noticing him too and darted off toward Dusty to greet him. Peyton dashed right after him and managed to grab the puppy right before he got a taste of freedom and gave him a choke hold while he headed back to the safety of his sandbox.

"Bad poppy," Peyton scolded him, watching the dog's ears lower down in submission. Patience laid down all of one second when his vision caught hold of something calling him to the water. Being energetic and eight months old now, Patience didn't like being cooped up very long and decided to run away again, only this time toward the pool area where a floating tennis ball, bobbed up in down in the water.

"Patience," Peyton screamed and ran after him. The puppy dived into the water and dog-paddled its way toward the ball and Peyton immediately thought the puppy was in trouble and jumped in after him.

Peyton knew how to swim—mommy and daddy had been sending him to the YMCA for swimming lessons—and Peyton swept his way toward the puppy that was still dog-paddling its way en route for the ball. Peyton finally reached the puppy at last and yanked him by his collar. But on instinct, the puppy's back legs circled around and Peyton was too small and too inexperienced to properly control the rescue and the puppy ended up unintentionally dragging the boy down as it began its descent toward the steps of the pool. Peyton's head submerged instantly, but then his little body popped back up again only to surrender to his modest arms that gave way to all the energy that was being expelled to breathe. His arms were failing fast as he struggled to keep up, but his efforts were unmet and Peyton dismally succumbed to the trouble.

Amber at first woke up from the screaming; a high-pitched shriek that was painstakingly hurting her ears. It was Mrs. Lopez...and that noise was coming from her? Amber noticed her on the other side of the pool—not in it, but beside it—with her hands to her face, screaming and carrying on, making a fuss about something...but, why?

She was only gone for five minutes! She only went into the house to get the boy some sun-screen, when Mrs. Lopez noticed the puppy drenched from being in the water and then observed a dark object at the bottom of the pool. A fright so intense, spread through to her skin, "Ah mi dios! Mi bebé de piscine! El bebé!"

In doubt, her body froze and not two seconds later, Amber watched Dusty come out of nowhere and dives into the deep end. **Did he even ask to go swimming—how rude of him,** she thought as she found her feet at last to stand up to follow his path in the water. Her heart dropped and in slow motion, Amber watched Dusty as he suddenly came up to the surface with an obvious bundle inside his arms with what looked like...a body?

OH MY GOD!

Amber collapsed to the ground almost immediately. Her intoxication along with her over exertion caused her to faint within viewing her little boys' dead body.

Mrs. Lopez finally turned around to find Mrs. Sanchez passed out on the concrete; she then gazed around to watch Dusty as he tried to retrieve Peyton by administering First Aid.

The little boy was pale and blue on his chest, face and lips. He was not breathing, there was no pulse and he couldn't feel a heartbeat. Of all the days! Of all the Goddamn days! Between breaths, Dusty voiced, "Call an ambulance!"

Mrs. Lopez' feet wouldn't move! Her shoes felt heavy and plastered to the ground but she nodded her head from the instruction and ran into the house as fast as she could where she dialed 9-1-1 and then sadly for Mr. Sanchez.

Eduardo was in the middle of a meeting with Stacey, Philip, Gordon and Martin. His face went white with alarm within hearing the news; at first, he choked back tears then five seconds later, ran out of the office to throw up his lunch.

# CHAPTER **SIXTEEN**

Eduardo met with the Los Angeles Deputy District Attorney at his office first before heading off to visit the Los Angeles County Coroner. Amber was at home however, but on the verge of being charged with child neglect and child endangerment.

In the past, Eduardo had worked with the district attorney over the years and had many friends and associates within the city. His familiarity with the municipality and his personal association with the District Attorney himself gave him partiality. Without a doubt, Amber would have been taken into custody immediately to be arraigned. But since Eduardo Sanchez, Esq. was already a public figure, his reputation spotless, the Deputy District Attorney and the City of Los Angeles decided **not** to file charges against his wife; cause of death was ruled an 'accidental drowning'.

Eduardo came home with hollowness in his heart and pain so extreme; the circumstances could never be really healed. Seeing his little boy naked and flat, motionless and unresponsive on that cold impersonal tabletop at the morgue all but broke his spirit to live. It was heart-wrenching to say the least and no parent should ever have to make funeral arrangements for a child.

He walked tediously up the staircase and opened up his bedroom door to find Mrs. Lopez and the dog by Amber's bedside. She was curled up in a fetal position and crying uncontrollably. Patience wagged his tail within seeing Eduardo enter and Mrs. Lopez grabbed him by his collar and headed out the door silenced by Eduardo's ruined expression.

Eduardo stood at the foot of the bed, staring at his wife with horrible, unimaginable, vile thoughts flooding through his principles.

He couldn't believe his wife couldn't stay sober enough to watch her own son! How could he ever forgive her? Oh dear God, he **hated** her at that moment. He wanted to beat her senseless, punch someone unconscious. He walked over to the floor length mirror and shoved his fist through the glass. Blood ripped through scrapes on his knuckles at once. He stood static, his chest slicing open from the sheer suffering and fell to his knees and buried his face in his blood soaked hands. A loud wail finally escaped his grief stricken mouth; terror so all consuming invaded his cry. "Why!" He shouted at her now, "Just tell me **why!**"

Amber opened her eyes at last and noticed Eduardo crotched down crying like a baby. Blood dripping from one of his hands—Good Lord, what did he do? She didn't realize the sound of glass shattering was the cause of him hitting the mirror with his fist. Amber thought it was just part of this recurring nightmare. She was at a loss for words. No possible logical explanation for any of it—her constant paranoia? Believing in her heart that her husband was attracted to another female, therefore, it was merited for her continued drunkenness? Were those good reasons for neglecting a child? It was a horrible mistake and accident—an irreversible act. Incomprehensible and preposterous, how could a mother be that careless and selfish? There really wasn't one excuse she could come up with—to place the blame on him? If he weren't so distant lately, so mysterious in his guise, so preoccupied with **something**, Amber wouldn't be so crazy to find out what was exhausting all his attention. "You're just as much to blame."

Eduardo remained squatting and wiped the blood on his expensive suit repeatedly. **"I'm** to blame?" He sourly expressed in a nauseated tone.

"If you had just admitted the truth in the beginning then maybe I wouldn't have required being numb half the day!"

Eduardo sat there with his mouth wide open. He wanted to attack her. He **undesired** her now. She became repulsive and sickening. He didn't even want to be in the same room with her! Enraged, he stood up and went to the closet to retrieve a single suitcase from the corner. He grabbed suits, shoes, ties, shirts and piled them high on a nearby stool. He flung a couple shoes clear across the room in a sudden fit of wrath. "I have not been unfaithful to you **once**!"

**"Liar!"** She screamed back at him, sitting straight up in the bed now. "Lusting after another woman other than your wife **is** cheating! And **I know you**," she laughed ironically, "I know your nature, you're a sexual predator, Eduardo and it was only a matter of time you bastard when you would have committed adultery...you've done it before!"

Eduardo stood defenseless. It was all true. Every single solitary bit of her accusation. He had been lusting after Stacey; at work, at home, Stacey depleted all his thoughts. He used to be a manic playboy, dating and bedding women left and right—and adultery? Oh, he couldn't deny that either; Amber was the woman he had the affair with.

They stared at each other for the longest time—Amber suspended in her justification—Eduardo draped in his condemnation.

Eduardo assaulted his clothes once more and shoved the bundle into his suitcase. "I'm staying at a hotel," he quietly mouthed heading out the doorway. "I'll let Mrs. Lopez give you the information at the funeral."

Peyton Enrique Sanchez, age four, had been buried at Forest Lawn in West Los Angeles. Death of a loved one is hard to grasp; the loss of a relative even more so, but to outlive your child—to lose a child to a tragic, violent death—was incomprehensible, even for Amber and Eduardo Sanchez.

Amber was in a daze; her perception hovered over her body like a cloud in the sky. Staring at the small coffin in the center of the aisle piled high with exquisite sprays of orchids and roses, Amber tried to imagine what it was like to be in that box. This might have been her destiny; a funeral, a coffin, her mother and sister weeping. This should have been her. This wasn't happening! It was all a demented monstrosity. She was going to wake up any moment now and feel her little boy within her arms again!

Wake up dammit!

Wake the hell up!

Eduardo sat on the opposite side of the pew along with his mother, and more surprisingly, his father and brother. He wanted no part of his wife at the moment, no part, but the little part that they had created.

Amber had been surrounded by her mother and sister while unfamiliar mourners passed her by to whisper their condolences. She heard nothing, but nodded her head as if she did and continued to stare eerily at the casket...**Her little boy lying inside. He didn't belong there. He didn't mean to die! Oh Good Lord, he couldn't breathe! Oh God, Peyton was inside that box. Oh Good Lord, he couldn't breathe!**

Amber sprang from her seat and hurled her body toward the chest. Anxiously, like a deranged lunatic she tried to unbolt the box. Gasps and shocks were heard throughout the congregation. The priest as well was in utter shock at the sight of the mother hurling the arrangement of flowers on top of the casket that skidded jarringly onto the tiled floor.

Eduardo immediately reacted to her exploit and yanked her body away before she unlocked one of the latches. He naturally pulled her body close to his and Amber impelled his comfort away. They stood center stage now—a pair in agony, a couple divided and that's when Amber slapped Eduardo across his face.

"Get the fuck away from me!" She bawled, pushing his body into another direction.

Sheila, Molly and Madge all swarmed Amber at that moment and guided her outside of the church.

Eduardo turned around and then sadly eyed all the patrons all staring back at him. Some of them bowed their heads, others shook them, but most of the mourners just grabbed hold of his heartache and grieved alongside with him. He turned to look at the coffin one more time and then stepped into his son to lay both hands on the wood as if he could heal him and cause him to rise. Feeling grief he never experienced before or after, at that moment he let go of his misery in front of all to witness.

# CHAPTER SEVENTEEN

Eduardo moved out of the house temporarily and into a hotel. Observing Amber drink herself into oblivion daily was not his idea of comfort. He'd rather remove himself from view than continue to scrutinize his wife as she withdrew from life. The child that they thought joined them together was now gone, therefore, what linked them mutually had vanished. It was do-or-die time. All or nothing, but how do you keep the music playing when all you keep hearing is a child's cry?

One o'clock in the morning and Amber was still up. How could she sleep when she knew her child was dead? The Vodka wasn't helping at all. One entire bottle tackled and she wasn't even drunk yet. Oh, she was numb to a degree, but in order for her to pass out, she required at least two full bottles dissipated.

She got up from bed and headed downstairs to the kitchen to fetch herself another decanter. She was just about to turn the kitchen light on when the doorbell rang. One o'clock in the morning and there was someone at the door?

Amber walked around the corner to the kitchen and down the long hallway that led to the front entry. There were iron gates surrounding the entire property, how in the hell did someone get in?

**Good Lord**, Amber thought, as she finished looking through the peephole. She opened up the door to find her husband tired and lost. "What are you doing here?" Amber asked, speaking to him through a crack in the doorway.

"I'm here to talk. Can I come in?"

Amber gazed down at the ground and then slowly up to survey his attire. Eduardo was still dressed in his best suit apparel, long black camel coat and silk tie and looked as if he had just come from work.

She opened up the door to let him in. "Our situation hasn't changed," she said under her breath.

Eduardo removed his coat and then laid it on a chair near the doorway. His demeanor appeared as if he were about to stay awhile. He inspected his wife, she was wearing lavender silk pajamas and the pink tone in her face hadn't gone away yet, therefore, she hadn't drunk herself into forgetfulness. "Can we go upstairs?"

Amber's heart sunk. The innuendo in her husband's eyes said it all. He **desired** her. He deliberately came over at one o'clock in the morning to make love to her? It had been eight months since they last kissed, eight long meticulous months since he was within.

Amber took hold of his hand and led him upstairs to their bedroom. Once there, Eduardo closed the door and began to unravel his tie. Amber closed the space between them and ran her hands up his chest. Oh how she missed his hard physique! Her breathing became more erratic as she gazed up into his eyes to grab hold of his stare and his parted lips. She knew he wanted to devour her but he held back.

"Come back to me," he whispered softly to her, kissing her lightly on the lips. Eduardo ran his fingers through her raven tresses and captured the back of her head, pulling her into his tongue and burning passion.

Amber forged them to bed and Eduardo brought down her silk camisole and exposed her breasts to his outburst and enthusiasm. Amber ran her hands down his bareback to his sinewy buttocks and pressed him against her heat—if he wanted her this badly she wasn't going to disappoint him. She unbuckled his belt and pulled his pants down at last. Amber tore his head away from her nipples and tightly wrapped her arms around his neck and back molding her wide-open mouth to his zeal.

Eduardo savored every sweet sensation he had with his wife. God, how he loved to make love to her! Her skin so soft, her body welcoming and perfect, and the way she made him feel when he was in her depths, sucking him in deeper and deeper advancing him to an unimaginable orgasm.

They lolled together unmoving in the slightest; languidly allowing the euphoria to pass. Normally, Eduardo would continue to kiss his wife with further ardor and she would welcome another encounter, but on this night, Eduardo quickly got off her body and lied down next to her staring up at the ceiling with his hand over his forehead.

Nothing had changed. How could the best of lovers be the best of friends? How do you muddle through the worst of agony and find a slight bit of happiness? Peyton was **still** gone and Amber **still** required being drunk half the day and Eduardo hated weakness. Loving each other wasn't enough for them. Reality ripped through their fantasy world and neither one knew how to make the first move.

Sex was a momentary diversion. Haunting memories came flooding back in huge tidal waves full of pain and accusations. Eduardo covered himself up with the blanket and decided rest was better now than arguing. He would wait till morning to see if things had changed between them. He rolled over on his side and away from Amber and closed his eyes.

Amber's eyes swelled with tears. She wanted to go down to the kitchen to grab another bottle, but then decided not to.  She too rolled over to her side of the bed and away from her husband, closing her eyes and silently cried herself to sleep.


The next morning, Eduardo awoke to sunshine in his face and uneasiness in his system.  He sat up and noticed Amber was no longer next to him.  He was just about to get out of bed when she appeared in the doorway with a champagne glass full of pink bubbly in her hand.  He stared at her for the longest time and then shut his eyes.  Good God, she was not willing to bend.  "I see you've had breakfast," Eduardo callously stated, whipping the sheet off his naked body and finding his boxer shorts and drawing them up.

"I woke up this morning and felt..." Amber stopped, feeling her throat close up, "happy for a second.  Then I remembered what day it was and that my son wasn't in his room...I needed a drink to cope with reality."

"What happened to us Amber?" He suddenly yelled at her, "Where's that unbreakable bond we were always talking about?"

"It died," she whimpered, "...it's buried in the ground with our son."

Eduardo watched his wife as she poured the liquid down her throat in one quick gulp like it was nothing.  All his life he had been a spoiled man, what he usually wanted, he usually got; but what he **wanted now** was for Amber to stop drinking!  She refused to bend and even tomorrow was a day wasted and he couldn't wait for his wife to get out of her slump.  He wanted comfort **now** and his wife was unable to supply it.

She physically changed right before his very eyes.  When Amber was intoxicated, she became this repulsive individual, her skin tone turned ashy, her hazel eyes turned near black, she slurred, she stumbled until she eventually passed out.

"Look at you, you're disgusting," he disclosed, picking up his clothes off the floor.

Amber was sloshed and enraged and ran toward the mirror. "For better—or for worse Eduardo, that's what a marriage is—for better or for worse. Right now I think we've officially reached the deep shit of hell," she exclaimed, grabbing scissors from a nearby drawer. She then raised the scissors to her head and began cutting away her hair and by the time she was done it was totally uneven and straggly all around her face. She looked like dreadful grunge, like some weird Tim Burton character in one of his movies. "I know I don't look so hot," she complained, "And maybe I never did," she broke down, waiving the scissors at her face and neck, "Oh I tried to be your Barbie Doll, I really did, but as much as I tried, I will never be a blond, never be perfect like most of the women you've dated—I'll always be this tall geeky insecure girl, who never felt as if she really fit in."

Eduardo was just standing there frozen; his only aspiration for her **now** was for her to pass out. "Is that what you think I want?" He yelled back at her grabbing the scissors away from her hand and tossing them into the trash. He then stomped over to the closet and yanked his last suitcase out. "I don't want some perfect woman Amber; I just want my wife back! I want how she used to make me feel, I want how she used to look—"

"She's gone," Amber slurred, beginning to feel lethargic from the alcohol, "she's gone with Peyton...with her 'lil boy...that woman is dead. **She's** to blame...**she's** at fault...she can never forgive herself for not staying sober enough to pay enough attention to him. I can't stop drinking...I can't...I won't because it helps me cope wif' my pain."

Eduardo began to pack his belongings. Suits, ties, shoes, socks and boxers all get thrown into one huge suitcase all over again—the rest of everything—until the closet was bare of any and all male occupation. "I feel grief too Amber and you don't see me drowning in two bottles of Vodka a day!"

Amber clutched the empty bottle in her hand and chucked it at her husband's head. Eduardo's reflexes act immediately and duck from the sight of the bottle hurling at his face.

"I want to stay numb," she whined, "...I want some'ne to **freeze me**...I no longer want to be strong, I want to sur'ender, I want a divorce."

Eduardo didn't know why but he almost felt relieved. The rope, the bond, the chain that kept them together was suddenly liberated. He wanted to comfort her, coddle her, but she kept pushing him away. "Fine, send the papers."

Amber stood by the window now, almost at the brink of her anesthetized slumber, "You'll be 'earing from my attorney."

Eduardo gripped his suitcases and turned to look at his wife one last time before he left. What happened to them? What became of the great compromise? What took over the love he once felt for her? He felt nothing but suffering; distress from Peyton's death and mental anguish from Amber's withdrawal. "You'll be hearing from mine."

Amber turned to look at her husband one last time and could instantly feel Eduardo's cold heart. The love she used to see through his green eyes alone ... vanished.

As soon as Eduardo stepped out from Amber's view, he leaned back against the hallway wall and bent over in torment. Tears swarmed his eyes instantly and he felt nothing but remorse and regret.

Saving face...why was that so burdensome? Why do **sorry** and **I need you** and *I love you* always have to be the hardest words to ever express?

# Chapter EIGHTEEN

"Harry **Balls**-son," Eduardo jokingly asserted, walking over to the man and greeting him.

"Ed-**weirdo**," Harry replied in his best Spanish accent, shaking his friend's hand.

"Don't tell me you're Amber's attorney?" Eduardo asked, shaking his head, "When did they let you out?"

"Fifteen minutes ago, I ran over here as fast as I could."

Eduardo started to laugh. He knew Harry from a long time ago and was surprised Amber remembered who he was. A high-powered Beverly Hills divorce attorney, Harry was known for hitting below the belt when it came to alimony. Many a famous actress was his clientele. He had been incarcerated for harboring a fugitive for two years though; Eduardo was truly staggered to see him free. "So she subbed out her pathetic counsel?"

"Got the call just yesterday, you don't mind, do you?"

"Why should I be? You're the best, and I expected nothing less from her. Have you met my counsel yet? Harry Billson, this is Tim Sinclair, Tim—Harry."

The two men shake hands and all three were about to enter the courtroom when Eduardo pulled Harry back.

"Before we go in Harry, can I speak to you...alone?"

"I highly oppose of this Eduardo," Tim suddenly said.

"I know—I know, it'll be just a second," Eduardo stated, wrapping his arm around his old friend and leading him away from his own counsel.

"What's on your mind? It can't possibly be about me being unethical and stealing that get out of jail free card."

Eduardo gave out a chuckle, "No, this is about my soon to be ex-wife."

"I'm listening."

"I'm not going to reject any offer that you place on the table Harry," Eduardo confessed, feeling his heart swell up with emotion. "I may not like my wife right now...she's done some pretty unforgivable things, but I'll always care for her and I want to make sure she's taken care of financially."

Harry stared at him agape. "Do you realize what you're saying? She could walk away with most of your fortune."

"I know—but you see, I'm in the position to make more, and she isn't. I vowed that I would always see to it that she was well cared for and I can't break that promise."

Harry shook his head. "In all my years Eduardo, I have never come across an ex-husband who **wanted** to take care of his ex-wife. It's kill or be killed where divorce is concerned. I take it Amber doesn't know about your sudden burst of knighthood?"

Eduardo doesn't laugh this time, "No—no she doesn't, and I'd rather keep it kind of discreet. So, whatever it is, come at me with all your ammunition, would you?"

"Absolutely—consider this war."

Harry hugged Eduardo and they both turned toward the courtroom. Eduardo noted his counsels discerning look and shrugged the guy off on his way in.

Amber was already seated at the table and didn't look at Eduardo as he sat down at the opposite end. It was a few months later and Amber had cut her hair off completely and looked more like a boy than some natural beauty.

The judge swore the session in and Harry went first. "Petitioner will now be seeking...forty thousand dollars monthly alimony, for five consecutive years, up and until she remarries."

Amber's eyes go wide. **That's not what was in the agreement!** What the hell did he just do? She thought they agreed on a much lesser amount. What the hell was going on? Did he just add an additional thirty thousand to the ten she originally asked for? She tugged at her attorney's jacket, "Harry, what the hell are you doing? Don't get him angry, please, he already agreed to the ten grand a month."

Harry bent over and whispered back to her, "Trust me love...I'm going to be your hero when this is over."

"Your Honor," Tim finally chimed in, "The decision of alimony has already been agreed upon, why is Petitioner's counsel suddenly raising the sum?"

The judge turned and gave Harry a sharp look. "Mr. Billson, you care to clarify?"

"Just realized something your Honor...Mrs. Sanchez needs to continue her life of luxury. When Mr. and Mrs. Sanchez were married, Mr. Sanchez demanded that Mrs. Sanchez quit her job and stay home to raise their young son. He explained to her that she would become a woman of leisure, his words, not mine—and she never had to work again. I believe Mrs. Sanchez deserves the increase to continue the life that's she been accustomed."

Eduardo leaned over and whispered something to his attorney; Amber could see him in the corner of her eye doing so. His counsel seemed upset and angrily whispered something back in return.

Tim cleared his throat, "It seems Respondent has had an epiphany of some sort and agrees to the forty thousand a month alimony."

Amber's jaw dropped to the table. What the hell was Eduardo doing? Amber sat there in awe as her attorney stated back and forth her demands, while Eduardo's attorney began to agree with every single one of them: The house, their three cars, the dog and all the furniture, winter vacation homes in Tahoe and Aspen, a time-share in Kauai, fifty-five percent holding interest in all of Eduardo's business investments and that ridiculous amount of forty thousand dollars a month?

Amber suddenly buried her head within her hands and realized now what her ex-husband was trying to do. He didn't want Amber to leave without making sure she was at least a little bit happy. Trying to concede and leave on happy terms; trying to ease any future pain. But she didn't want to be taken care of anymore; she just wanted to run away. Die alongside Peyton.

She yanked at Harry's lapel again and cut short his further claims in midsentence. "I don't want it," she said feeling her heart pound uncontrollably.

He looked at her as if she just lost her fuckin' mind. "Mrs. Sanchez," he hushed down, "Amber...what part don't you want?"

Amber stared at him serious, "Any of it."

Harry's eyes grew wide, "What?" He let go bewildered. "I'm afraid I can't let you do that."

"Why not?" Amber suddenly raised her voice, looking at the judge now; making sure her choice was loud and clear. "I don't want it, I don't want his money, and I don't want his property. I don't want anything. I just want a divorce...and the dog, I want to keep the dog."

Eduardo gazed over at Harry and his soon to be ex-wife. His heart was suddenly being pulled from all directions. What the hell was she doing? Amber wanted **nothing?**

Harry suddenly spoke up after shaking his head a couple of times, "Your Honor...Petitioner is withdrawing all appeals."

The judge stared at him astounded. Eduardo just shut his eyes. Damn her. She really did want to cut all ties.

Amber stood up and then stormed out of the courtroom, Kleenex in hand, wiping away her tears that were gushing down her face. Eduardo stood up and then darted out after her, but she was too quick and seemed to disappear in the crowds of people exiting out through the glass doors.

Later, Eduardo found Harry waltzing along the corridor.

"Harry..."

Harry turned around and gazed in to his friends eyes. He was just as disbelieving as he was, "I had no idea Eduardo. I didn't know she was going to request such ridiculous legal recourse."

"Would you do something for me?"

"Sure, anything."

"Set up a trust account. Set it up in her mother's name, Sheila Thomas. Amber's mother will be the Executor to her estate, I trust her with my money. I'll send her the forty grand each month."

Harry just stood there agape, "Eduardo, can I ask you something?"

"Sure—anything."

"Why are you getting a divorce?"

Why? Why was he divorcing her? Why was he walking away from the only woman he ever truly loved? Did their relationship die when their son did? "Harry, if I knew the answer to that we wouldn't be here now, would we?"

Eduardo actually waited until the divorce papers were legally stamped "recorded" when he finally approached Stacey's door.

"Can I come in?"

Stacey was in the middle of reading a book, but Eduardo Sanchez suddenly crowding her doorway was a way better option for the evening, "Absolutely."

Eduardo walked in, but remained hesitant. Stacey studied his eyes for a moment and decided a drink was in order.

"Would you like a glass of brandy?"

Eduardo's throat closed up, his heartbeat escalated...Good God, he was nervous? He hadn't been on the prowl for a very long time and it felt awkward to be alone with another woman knowing his only intention was to bed her. To be honest, he wondered what Amber was doing at that moment and pined away for her and her presence. What was she doing now? The house had been sold three months earlier and he had to let go of Mrs. Lopez, there really was no need for a nanny any longer, and the last he heard, Amber had moved to the valley and into an apartment somewhere near the foothills. Eduardo continued to stay by the beach and bought a townhome in Malibu. All their past acquaintances had been severed too, he not only divorced his wife, but he divorced their friends as well.

He gazed over at Stacey and felt guilt running through his veins. He would be using her, plain and simple. Would she mind? Would she even care? Or would she simply relent from the sheer joy of getting exactly what **she's** longed for?

He downed the remaining brandy in his glass then gave Stacey a sweltering look. He watched her place down hers as well and that was all the confirmation he needed. He stepped into her and closed the space between them. Circling his green eyes around her milky white skin first, he thought "I love my wife" and grabbed Stacey into his arms and kissed her passionately.

Eduardo started to undress her and Stacey did the same; two bodies in a heated impatient choreography. He unraveled his tie, unbuttoned his shirt, she unzipped her dress, unhooked her bra. Eduardo darted in towards her neck; she kissed his chest sensuously until they found their way to the bed.

Stacey couldn't believe it, it was what she had dreamt about for the past twenty years. He was finally filling her, ramming her and oh God he was so big and wonderful, everything she always fantasized he would be like and he didn't disappoint. Stacey closed her eyes as Eduardo continued to make love to her and Stacey relished every luscious second.

Later, Eduardo woke up in a cold sweat. Sitting up in bed, he threw his legs over to the side and sat on the edge of the bed. Feeling sweat dripping off the center of his back and neck, he turned to look over at Stacey; she was sleeping soundly with a smile pasted to her face.

"At least someone's happy," he muttered to himself, drawing up his boxer shorts and roaming over by the windowsill.

It was winter in California and the rain pounded hard onto the glass, tapping at the window like someone wanting to get in. He stood still and gazed out at the storm and instantly brought to mind what rainy days always reminded him of; his ex-wife.

He went to drop off Adrian's Disney video in the middle of the night and was suddenly caught off guard by Amber still being awake. God, her arrival was nothing short of spectacular! She had flung the door open to his prurient universe, enticing not only his body, but his very mind and soul. Good God, he loved her then...Good God, he loved her still! Good God, what the hell did he just do? He just had sex with a gorgeous blond and he was feeling nothing but remorse? Only one emotion could contribute to the feeling that he was having. Guilt. Never in his wildest imagination did he believe he'd be making love to another woman other than Amber for the rest of his life. Amber was his soul mate, the woman he felt finalized with. Why did he just have sex with Stacey? He felt sick all of a sudden, nauseated.

He walked over to the bathroom and turned on the faucet to splash cold water in his face, but then leaned over the wash-basin to throw up. He was sick, he was tormented, or was he really ill? He felt like death warmed over and looked at himself in the vanity mirror. He **looked** like death warmed over.

He unexpectedly stiffened up when he felt Stacey's hands running up and down his back; caressing his shoulders, his waist down to his groin. He turned around and looked sharply in her eyes. He felt sick again, he's never been this afflicted before!

"You OK?" She asked, watching him dart toward the toilet to throw up the rest of the brandy.

Eduardo hugged the toilet bowl, "No, just go back to bed Stacey, I think I just ate something bad."

Stacey started to exit within hearing Eduardo vomit once more.

She closed the door behind her and guessed having sex over and again was out of the question?

# CHAPTER **NINETEEN**

A few months later, the routine began to get a little bit easier. No more sobbing on the way there, only some stifled emotion as he drove through the wrought-iron gates.

Eduardo arrived at the cemetery midday. He got out of car and slowly emerged the area where his little boy had been. As soon as he reached the gravesite, he stared down at the headstone.

*Peyton Enrique Sanchez*

*Our Miraculous Son*

*Mommy and Daddy Will Always*

*Love You*

He started to choke back tears again and knelt down to admire the various flowers that surrounded his son's gravesite. It was Peyton's birthday—he would have been five.

There were flowers from his own mother, his former mother-in-law, Peyton's Aunt Molly, and...Good God, could it be—a wrapped present hidden behind the bouquets with a card that read, "Love Mommy."

Tears ran down his face at once as he picked up the present and gazed up and around him. Amber was nowhere in sight but she had obviously been there and a strange pang was felt deep within his heart because he had missed her so. No, that wasn't the complete truth, he missed her a lot; being around her, hearing her voice and being able to touch her daily. He looked down at the present again and felt compelled to open it. He wanted to see what she got him. What an awful horrible feeling! What the hell happened to them? Was it really Peyton's death that had broken them apart? Or was it something else entirely? They never really did get a chance to heal. He just accused her—she just blamed him—and no one was sane enough to bend, or were they doomed from the very beginning, marrying his brother's wife; some kind of divine retribution, punishing them for their retched sins?

Eduardo knelt back down and placed the present back on top of his son's grave. He suddenly felt compelled to see Kyra, his daughter from his first wife Leticia. Eduardo then placed the present he brought for his son next to Amber's just before he left.

He arrived shortly after at Leticia residence, at the home he had bought with her when they were married. He really didn't want to take care of **her**, but felt it was necessary for his daughter to continue living in comfort; a four-bedroom, three bath home right smack in the middle of a posh part of Encino, California.

He knocked on their front door then waited a few seconds until Leticia suddenly appeared with her blond highlights and upgraded bosom.

Leticia Sanchez was still tall and still beautiful with stunning green eyes similar to Eduardo's. She was still single and still resentful and judged her ex-husband up and down as if he were some riff-raff off the street. After their divorce, Leticia joined a "Why Men Cheat" women's healing group and tried to get over her ex-husband, but could not. The depression was madness and full of loneliness and Leticia then signed up for Match.com. It didn't work; everyone that she dated was then hopelessly compared to her ex-husband so Leticia sent Kyra off to stay with her parents and flew off to Cabo San Lucas for some rest and relaxation (i.e., some mindless sex). Having only slept with one man (her ex-husband) her entire life, she bedded the first man she came across and woke up the next morning with the waiter she met at the hotel restaurant. He was fifteen years younger than she and Leticia felt more like a tramp than some cougar when she learned of his age and sent him on his way. Two days later, she hooked up with another man, some television actor on vacation and he sent her on her way. One night stands simply weren't for her and decided when she returned to the states, she was going to go back to church and find a good Catholic mate. There wasn't one; they were too old, married and too young or had a fear of commitment. She just couldn't get over that ex-husband! She felt blind-sided, she had no clue and Eduardo had always acted the same when he was around the family. He always gave her the attention that she had craved and made love to her when she needed the intimacy; she just missed being with him. Oh, she hated being single and hated feeling this way constantly and decided to redo her self-image and started with her self-esteem. Large breasts; she always wanted them and what better way to spend her ex's money than to get breast implants? She always hated having small breasts and opted towards the Pam Anderson's. But when the plastic surgeon explained to her that Leticia's back wouldn't be able to sustain that much weight, she chose the Carmen Electra's instead.

Leticia hated Eduardo with a passion now...no, that wasn't entirely true, she still loved him and it hurt her to see him so happy living without her. "Come to see our child? Now that your prized son has passed?" Leticia spitefully voiced, rapidly becoming ugly. "Finally realized you had another one?"

"Can I come in?" He asked, rolling his eyes away from hers.

"What makes you think I would let you in?" She remarked with a sneer.

"Because as much as you hate to admit it Leticia, I still fathered Kyra and I still have rights."

"Rights? Huh, that's a laugh, where were mine when that woman stole you away from me?" Leticia maliciously expressed, posing and arching her back.

Eduardo started to laugh at her obvious demonstration, "Now is not the time Leticia, now can I come in?"

"You're never allowed back into this house!" She snarled at him.

Eduardo was livid and was not in the mood. "Then send my daughter outside or I will drag your ass back into court."

Leticia hesitated; the last time Eduardo had taken her to court, she lost full physical custody and a reduction in alimony. She wanted no chance of that, in fact, she never could win against a great legal mind like Eduardo's—it was a losing game. "You can see her on one condition."

"You don't hold authority to option out any conditions Leticia, so if you and your silicone friends would just let me pass, I would like to see my daughter."

"You think I did this for you?" Leticia hooted, sticking out her new breasts for him to get a better look. "How conceited you are Eduardo! You really think you still maintain that much persuasion?"

Eduardo let go a devastating cocky grin and brought his eyes up and down her body, practically making love to her with his measured erotic scrutiny. "I do."

Leticia was breathless and signed heavily. He did, damn him. She kicked the door open with the back of her foot then watched as her ex-husband entered her home as if he still owned the place.

"Where is she?"

"She's upstairs doing her homework, I'll call her." Leticia suddenly felt incredibly sorry for her nastiness a little bit earlier and decided to rectify an out of control situation. "...Eduardo," she let go, feeling moisture at the back of her throat, "I'm so sorry to hear about Peyton."

Eduardo bent his head down and choked back his tears. He wasn't about to cry in front of **her**. "Thank you."

Just then, Leticia went for him, intending on embracing him, but Eduardo backed away from her approach.

"Don't touch me," he snapped back at her.

"I'm sorry, I just," she remarked, "...I just wanted to give you a hug."

Eduardo stared at his ex-wife. She was a stranger to him now. He never did love her. Leticia had gotten pregnant on their first night together. She was a virgin at the time, and he had no other choice but to marry her when she cried that he had compromised her. She was just a mistake, a costly mistake, but he's always loved his daughter. "I'm OK Leticia."

"No, you're not," she said convincingly, watching his shoulders slump. He was about to give into her comfort when Kyra, age ten, came skipping down the staircase.

"Daddy!" She screamed, running into his wide arms.

Eduardo hugged his daughter with a thunderous greeting and kissed Kyra on her forehead. She looked identical to him with the same color hair and green eyes. She was turning out to be such a sweet kid too. "How about spending some time with your dad?"

"Can I mom?" Kyra asked, her green eyes widening with anxiousness.

Leticia gazed over at Eduardo's quizzical face. "Sure," she let go, feeling resentful for not being invited.


Eduardo took Kyra to the Santa Monica pier where he knew she would enjoy herself on the Ferris wheel and carnival rides. Later, he was over-whelmed with how mature she seemed to him now, no longer the little girl when he last lived with her, but a pre-teen who was into Miley Cyrus, the Jonas Brothers, text messaging, roller blades, water slides, school, video games and, of course, boys. And Eduardo sat there tongue-tied through most of it while she rambled on and on about almost anything and everything and was so amazed at how much he truly missed and how much he truly missed being **someone's** parent.

# CHAPTER TWENTY

At the same time, Amber had the urge to visit Victor again, and as soon as he sees her, he tells her he won't watch her destroy herself. Victor explained to her that she needed to go seek medical treatment and that he wasn't going to allow the children to continue to see her unless she sought help.

Amber was turning into a "drunk", a person who required alcohol other than when socially. Victor shook his head as he sat down. He couldn't believe she was still drinking.

"You need to stop," he told her, smoothing down an area next to him so that his pregnant wife could take a seat. Josie was pregnant again with their second child. "Sit here baby."

Amber eyed his wife as she hobbled on over and sat close to him. Lowering her eyes, she looked down at the ground before eyeing the television set. Could she do it? Stop the numbing process that seemed to help in the beginning, but no longer did. What else could she do or take to help cope with the throbbing? Vodka was easy and it helped satisfy her quench to be constantly medicated...would pills do the trick?

Amber blinked out of her daze for a moment and eyed the television set once again. Focusing on a newsbreak, her eyes widened on the face of her now ex-husband. It was Eduardo at a news conference; he was being interviewed as part of a celebrity case involving Yazmine whose trial finally began.

Victor noted Amber's reaction to the update, "Do you want me to change the channel?" He asked her with the remote control already in position to do so.

Amber reached out her hand for him to stop, "No, don't change it. I'm over him; it doesn't hurt so much anymore."

Victor let go a chuckle, **yah right.**

Amber scanned over Eduardo like just another viewer watching a commercial...and then she sees her. The blond in the back of him...to the right of him, actually, standing vigil, standing proud...and clearly, the winner; Barbie and Ken come to mind, as Amber silently watched the two on them on the television screen.

Victor kept eyeing his ex-wife as she stared blankly at the box.

Amber simply stared at the screen. Simply staring at him and her...him **with** her and her heart began to pound a little faster. Several inches shorter than Eduardo, Stacey was the epitome of blond supremacy. Long flaxen hair, bright sky blue eyes, tan supple skin, a voluptuous physique. She was even an attorney—that meant she possessed a brain and simultaneously, Amber envisioned the two of them kissing. Good Lord, the image wouldn't blink away! "Victor, you have something to drink?"

Victor stared at her in awe, "Beer, but you can't have it."

Amber stood up then stared down at him and contemplated raiding his refrigerator, "Why not?"

Victor stood up with her, intending on beating her to the kitchen if she even tried, "Because Amber, look at you, you're a mess. You need help."

Amber darted toward the kitchen but Victor beat her to the frig. He hovered over the refrigerator like a pirate over his gold. "Don't you dare."

Amber reached for the handle, "I need a drink! Let me have at least one beer, please Victor, it's only one beer!"

Victor stayed his ground, "No Amber, you need help, I'm calling your mother."

Amber wasn't scared, "I don't care, go and call her—I'll even give you the number! Now move away, I need a drink."

Victor pushed toward her and then grabbed at her waist to drag her out of the kitchen and back into the living room. Josie was in awe of the two of them making a spectacle of the situation and then eyed Valentina coming in through the front of their doorway.

"Mom!" Valentina cried, running towards her parents and grabbing at her father's hands to release her mom.

Victor let go of Amber instantly and Amber nearly toppled over, but grabbed her purse before setting eyes on her daughter. Not feeling any shame, she began her ascent toward the front door. "If you don't offer me a beer, then I'm leaving to the nearest bar."

Victor's mouth dropped open wide. "Then go," he ended up saying, feeling remorseful. "But Amber, I don't want my kids near you if you continue to drink," he relayed, grabbing Valentina to his chest and giving her fatherly squeeze. "Unless you get help, you're no longer welcome here."

Amber's mouth closed up and distress returned to her eyes. Again, her child was being taken away? Why were children always being used as a bargaining tool?! "Fine Eduardo," she let go realizing immediately what she just said.

Victor guffawed, "Its **Victor**."

Amber gazed over at the set once again and realized that her ex and his new someone were no longer part of the news. She bent her head down and left the house without a further word.

# CHAPTER TWENTY-ONE

"Hi, this is Madge—I'm out of country searching for a Latin husband and plan to return in two weeks, leave a message at the tone..."

Amber hung up the receiver and continued to stare out the window. She had been sitting alone in the dark until a twinkle of light beamed through from the full moon outside her window. Two bottles of SKYY and a nearby champagne glass occupy her dresser. She was glaring out the window; out at nothing and out at nowhere. She was dead inside. Love, life had escaped her and she hadn't eaten in almost a week. She was so distraught, so depressed, so...**tired**. She wanted to die again. Let it go. Set the pain free. She missed Peyton, missed her two other kids...missed...something she used to have...with that man.

She'd do anything to feel his body next to hers. Why couldn't he sense that she was in pain? It was all so crazy—and maybe she had been responsible. Eduardo had moved on and it had all been her fault—he had someone else to comfort him—all she had was heartache.

Good Lord, why couldn't the throbbing subside? She had been drinking non-stop for four consecutive days and nothing was helping!

She brought the glass up to her lips and gulped the remaining alcohol down. It spread throughout her veins and warmed her heart, but didn't take away the anguish.

She closed her eyes and instantly envisioned Eduardo holding Stacey with his long arms around her petite body. She was so beautiful...with her long blond platinum hair, those azure eyes flickering at the sight of Eduardo smiling down at her.

Good Lord, why couldn't she heal! It simply wasn't fair. He had someone to take away **his** pain, but she didn't have anyone! Her mother and sister were only temporary aids, with their words of encouragement and their love and their strength. Amber would feel good for a few short days until her mind would wander to when she was able to wrap her arms around the man she once loved and hold the little boy she once adored.

Eduardo lied to her again! He said he would always love her no matter what and that they had this connection that would never be broken...and where was that eternal bond now? Where was that forever love? Where was it hiding? Why'd it go away? Why couldn't she find it?

Amber got up only to fall to the floor and started to bawl from the continuous torment of Eduardo kissing Stacey inside her mind. Eduardo was bringing his hands up around her face, leaning into her and brushing her lips so tenderly. His touch, so divine, passion was dispensed instantly through his fingers alone.

Stacey was kissing him; she loved him through the night with Eduardo naked...his muscled chest heated against hers. She was tilting her head back in ecstasy, while Eduardo drove his pinnacle home.

Amber got up on all fours and started to crawl toward her bathroom. She was heaving from the consistent mental pictures and was trying to catch her breath, and trying...ever so hard...to just...be.

Amber reached her vanity at last and like a raving lunatic, pulled herself up and began her endless search for something sharp. Good Lord, where was that razor blade?!

Amber started hurling combs, brushes, tooth-paste, mirrors, curlers, makeup across the area. Searching, searching for a Goddamn razor blade! She wanted to end it, wanted to end it now.

Amber ran to the medicine cabinet, then started to heave all the prescription bottles onto the floor—nothing, zero, zilch. Goddamn Eduardo! He wouldn't get out of her head!

She then proceeded into the closet and eyed her belts hanging on a hanger. A belt. She could hang herself. Where? Amber emerged out of the closet looking up and around the bathroom. The shower? She could hang herself up on the spout. Would it hold her weight? No. She looked across and over above her bed. The ceiling fan, it was secure, it could hold her weight. She slowly stalked it and stood up on the bed then wrapped the belt around one edge and pulled down on it with all her might. Yes, definitely. It would hold her weight.

Amber bent over again and cried in her lap. So many memories dashed in and around her aching heart. Peyton, her baby boy, why did he have to die? He was just a little boy! He had his whole life ahead of him. What did he do? It was **she** who had been bad and therefore, punished. It was she. Her affair? Was she being punished for having an affair with Eduardo? Were they being punished for being...happy?

**Oh...dear...God,** her poor baby, all alone in that dark closed box. Feeling compelled to take a shovel and dig him out, he didn't belong there. Good Lord, she didn't have enough time with him. Why was **he** dead? She should be the one who should die!

Amber wrapped the other side of the belt around her neck then realized sickly that it wasn't long enough once she tied the knot. She fell down to the bed and wiped away her tears already streaming down the sides of her face when she noticed the bottles that were tossed on the floor when she was searching for a razor blade.

Asendin. Desyrel. Pamelor and Prozac for her depression. Dalmane, Seconal to help her sleep. **Yes. Yes, those will do.**

Amber got off the bed and picked up all the bottles off the floor and started to empty each and every one until there was a mound of prescription drugs on her mattress. She eyed the bottle of Vodka conveniently on the end table and walked over to it and brought it toward the bed. Without any hesitation, without any shame, Amber grabbed a handful of mixed pills and plopped them all in her mouth. She then brought the bottle up to her throat and took a swig of the liquid and then downed the rest of the Vodka.

No one saw him walking down the desolate corridor this time. Not one single nurse—or one single woman—had been captured by his attractive facade.

Eduardo reached Amber's bedside at two o'clock in the morning and slowly sat down next to her lying there. He was in awe—he was in disbelief, and lowered his head. What an awful sight, Amber numb in a hospital bed. How many months had he held vigil at her bedside when she tried to commit suicide once before? Sixteen painstaking months? Why did she do this again? Why did she feel that taking her life was always the answer?

He grabbed her hand, but didn't cry on her lap like the last time. He did however, smoothed his fingers over hers and thought about Mrs. Lopez. It was she who had notified him about Amber's latest attempt. He had no idea that when he let go of his nanny that she would run to Amber to see if she could help her and Amber hired her mostly for companionship and not to clean up her apartment. He guessed they had struck up a bond after all and that caused a weak smile to his lips.

Mrs. Lopez called an ambulance immediately when she found Amber out cold on her bed. Patience was right by her side once again and kept her body warm.

Amber had a gastric lavage or her stomach pumped within reaching the emergency room. Activated charcoal was then given to Amber to help absorb any drugs or poisons that were left in the stomach.

Eduardo was startled by Sheila and Molly walking in through the door at that moment, he didn't expect to see them there, especially so late at night. Standing up, he first straightened out his apparel.

Sheila and Molly were in shock. Of all people, they certainly didn't expect to see Eduardo, Victor maybe, but definitely not Eduardo.

"What are you doing here?" Sheila asked, speaking up first.

Eduardo looked over at Amber, she still wasn't awake. "Mrs. Lopez called me. She thought I'd want to know."

"And do you? Want to know I mean?" Sheila asked hopeful.

"Of course...**always,** excuse me," Eduardo expressed walking around the two gawking women and out the door.

"I can't believe he came, mom," Molly relayed, gazing over at Amber's body, "Do you think he still loves her?"

Sheila looked over at Amber herself. Amber was beginning to show signs of waking up. "We'll never know...will we?" Sheila then leaned down and grabbed at Amber's hand.

"I'm gonna find out," Molly slowly said, smiling at Amber as she stirred in the bed.

"But Amber will never know how he truly feels, not unless she stays alive."

Amber opened her eyes to find Sheila and her sister Molly at her side. They smile down at her as Amber painstakingly brought her hand up to her forehead.

"I'm mad at you," Sheila sternly pronounced holding back her tears.

Amber couldn't move her mouth; she couldn't believe she was still here! Good Lord, why didn't she die? "Who found me?"

"Mrs. Lopez. She wouldn't have been there, but she went back to your apartment to collect something she forgot. Patience was howling beside you on the bed."

"Oh mom...why didn't you just let me die?"

Sheila now let go of her anger and especially her emotion, "Because you're my daughter **dammit!** And I'm sick and tired of watching you destroy yourself! You've single handedly ruined your life Amber; a death of a child doesn't always equal a death of a marriage. You two should have held it together, not break it apart—it was just a test, couldn't you see that? You pushed away a man who adored you Amber and you threw away a marriage that **even I** wished I had. You're going back to Palm Desert Treatment Center whether you like it or not!"


"Eduardo!"

He turned around, shocked at the sight of his former sister-in-law running down the hallway toward him. "Molly? What happened...Is she OK?"

"Do you still love my sister?"

Eduardo turned to look down the hallway and the doorway he just came from, "I told you already, I'll always care for her, is she OK?"

Molly laughed, and then dug her hands in her back pockets. "Yes, she just woke up and looks as if she'll be fine."

Eduardo closed his eyes and then dug his own hands down his coat pockets. "Thank God."

Molly looked into his eyes as he raised them to look into hers. "Do you remember when Amber tried to get us together all those years ago?"

Eduardo remembered the day of Amber's wedding; it was the day Amber married his brother. Boy was that a tumultuous time. He didn't know if he was coming or going. He knew he was in love with her but never wanted to actually admit it. Just watching her intermingle within his family, kiss and hold his brother was pure torture.

At the wedding, Amber tried to set him up with her sister. They danced the remainder of the wedding reception, even went out for coffee later, Molly was very nice girl, but he simply wasn't interested. "Why?"

"Oh Eduardo, I knew back then that you cared for my sister. The way you used to look at her, I tried to deny it because I thought Amber was in love with Victor."

"Me too," he said, looking down at the ground.

"I don't understand it...God, I've been so jealous of what you two had! Look at me, I'll be forty this year and I haven't even gotten married yet. I date producers, actors, directors, cameramen, average Joe's off the street, but I can never seem to find not even a smidgen of what you two shared."

Eduardo stared at Molly. She was the same height as her sister, almost the same color hair, but her eyes were brown. He stared at her brown eyes for a second and then looked back at the ground. "Your sister is poison to me right now. I just need time away to sort things through. I, myself haven't even had a chance to grieve for my son," he said, his voice cracking. "It's been all about your sister—"

"Rather than all about you, right? Good heavens, if you're not the center of the universe, then no one else deserves to grab some attention?"

Eduardo swallowed his pride. Contempt, he hated condescension. "Your sister hates me Molly. **Hates me.**"

Molly started to howl, "My sister **worshipped** you! What a crazy proud fool you are...if you can't wait to get back what you had together then you don't deserve her."

Amber went back to Palm Desert Treatment Center and underwent her detox from drugs and alcohol. She met up with Dr. Hayward again and he was saddened by her return.

During the next couple of months, her one and one sessions consisted of Amber telling him about Eduardo and what happened to them. Confessions that included the reasons why she started to drink heavily and the excuses as to why; having an affair, coping with the ridicule. She told Dr. Hayward that she thought Eduardo was cheating on her and that he continued to deny it. She believed he was lying and that forced her to start to drink because the intuition was making her crazy.

And then there was Peyton. Her little boy often haunted her, waking up in the middle of the night, imagining him standing there at the edge of her bed, watching her sleep. She truly believed they lost Peyton because they were being punished for committing adultery. Dr. Hayward explained to her that it was simply not the case, that Peyton was a God send, not a sacrifice. They chose to destroy it, not some profound upper being choosing reckoning. Amber realized she continued to be numb from Eduardo abandoning her and she would never forgive him for that.

It was there that Amber learned to forgive, but Eduardo would never know that.

# CHAPTER TWENTY-TWO

## Another Year Goes By

What the heck does painting have to do with recovering from acute depression? Nothing, Amber realized as she plopped a dab of bluish paint onto a blank canvas. Two other patients were spread out amongst her and outside trying to paint the indigo sky.

Amber began to swish the paint around, making a mess rather than creating something artistic. She went to scratch her forehead and tried to figure out how to paint the ocean when a blob of blue paint fell onto her cheek. She grabbed a nearby cloth she had resting over the back of her chair and wiped the paint away from her face but didn't realize she had just made a noticeable blue streak across her skin. She continued on with her painting, dabbing the blue every which way but right.

"I'd buy that."

Amber turned around and was astonished by what she saw. She scanned over his legs first and brought her eyes gradually up to his face. He was tall, taller than Amber, she assumed. Her heart began to beat faster when her eyes reached his face. He was also very good-looking and...**Latin**, like her ex, Amber immediately turned back to her canvas with her face hot from an evident blush. "Thanks," she let go, "But it's not for sale, I'm thinking of giving it to Dr. Hayward as a wedding present."

"Trying to piss him off?"

Amber started to giggle, "That **was** my intention."

Anthony Rivera walked into her full view. She hadn't fully looked at him, but he noticed her. Her hair was quite striking; he always loved ebony hair on a woman. Her face, he didn't quite count on. She was unique in her genuineness. No makeup, she was a natural beauty with a matchless pair of eyes that seized the deal and that's when he realized he'd seen her somewhere before.

Amber's breath was taken away momentarily once he came into full light. No one had affected her heart that way since her ex husband, meeting this man was electric. The man was not only good-looking, but gorgeous on top; tall and distinctive looking with classic features, a goatee around his mouth, long thin nose and aquiline brown eyes. His hair was dark, black, almost like hers. He made her heart flutter.

"Tony Rivera, recovering alcoholic," he presented her, extending out his hand for hers to shake. When she went to shake his hand, he grabbed the cloth off her lap, and then wiped the remaining blue paint off her cheek that was blemishing her appeal.

He wasn't shy, she realized, rather bold of him to do that too. "Amber Sanchez, recovering from depression and fear of abandonment," she happily expressed, realizing how truly attractive he was.

Tony started to howl. "Dr. Hayward feed you that line?"

Amber smiled in return, blushed at his smile and the way he made her feel when it hit her. They had met before? "Do we know each other?"

Tony gazed around him and drew up a nearby chair and positioned it next to hers. He turned the chair around and leaned his broad arms and shoulders on the rim. "A long time ago," he softly said, his voice trailing, "And no longer matters."

Amber looked shyly away again. He really shouldn't be affecting her heart the way that it was but he did, "You were a business partner of ours, weren't you?" She asked, nodding her head, the images of that magical night all coming back to her. "We met at the bar?"

Tony was elated that she had remembered. "I told you were beautiful," he smiled, exposing his nice white grin. "You still are."

Amber let the compliment sink in. It sure felt good. "You new here?"

"No," Tony voiced, looking down at the grass, "I've been a patient on and off for the past several years. This has been the longest I've been sober though. I'm going on three years."

Amber soaked in his sadness, "That's wonderful, I'm happy for you."

Tony smiled; he really didn't expect to fully be engrossed by her, but she was wonderful. She was also easy to talk to and he wasn't the least bit nervous like he usually was around women he was physically attracted to and who the hell cared where they first met and who they were both linked to. "Thanks, I've come a long way."

"I've been here almost a year now," Amber confessed looking into his brown sincere eyes. "It's been rather difficult."

"I know."

Amber stared at him for a moment. Why was she so comfortable with him? "Of course you do."

"Have you eaten lunch yet?"

His words stumped her heart. **Those words**, that phrase, Victor had asked her that very same thing when she first met him! Was Tony brought back to her for companionship or something else entirely? Her heart began to beat a little bit faster because of that **something else**. A deep sense of comfort entered her heart, she

couldn't help but beam. Was Tony her guardian angel?
"No, I'm starving."

They sat across from each other for hours upon hours
and spilled their guts about other tidbits and about each
other's pasts. Tony wasn't surprised about Amber's
description of her outward appearance while she drank,
Tony had been the same way, only he was an ugly drunk;
mean, evil, menacing, and nasty. Anyone who got in his
way would either be threatened with physical harm, or
lashed out by his scorpion tongue.

Tony was now a successful engineer; several
downtown Los Angeles projects in the works, as well as
across the country and a few even in Europe. He was a
self-made millionaire at forty-two, divorced and downright
enchanted by Amber.

Amber was...cautious. Here was a man similar to
her ex. Tony spoke to her with authority, with intelligence,
with pride. There wasn't one attribute she didn't find
different about Tony other than his eyes and face.
Eduardo's were green and Tony's were brown, other than
that, he was nearly the same person! Physically, but by no
means compelling, Eduardo owned his sexual magnetism,
whereas Tony was shy and reserved about his
attractiveness.

Could Tony be the next man for her? Amber was
determined to find out. He was at the center for his yearly
follow-up with Dr. Hayward and was only going to be
staying at the Palm Desert Treatment Center for just a
week, but decided to stay longer.

And during this time, Amber and Tony were
inseparable. Talking about where they grew up, whom
they married, if they had any children. And that's when it
got painful. Tony had a daughter once. She died of
leukemia. She was only seven, and it drove him to drink.
Amber was instantly pulled in by their sudden
comparatives. She told him about Peyton, how she felt it

was her fault and how she thought she was being punished. They cried in each other's arms for hours, realizing how much they had in common and made love for the very first time.


They were walking hand-in-hand in through the palm tree gardens when Tony suddenly whipped her body around and embraced Amber passionately; kissing her with tender ardor. Amber was taken-back; it was the first time she had felt loved in over a year. She instantly felt Tony's passion, but she still couldn't find hers. What the hell was wrong with her? Was she still dead inside? She was a healthy woman, able to give and receive love and she still couldn't find that emotion?

"I'm in love with you Amber," Tony whispered in her ear as his hands freely roamed her backside.

Amber closed her eyes. Good Lord, she wanted to say it back, but she couldn't. She just couldn't!

"You don't have to say anything just yet," he let go picking up on her hesitation, "you don't even have to return my love. I just wanted you to know how much I care and what my intentions were. I want to marry you Amber Sanchez, will you marry me?"

Amber pulled apart from him. "Absolutely," she said, grabbing his face with both of her hands. "I could fall in love you Tony, I know I could. Will you accept my agreement knowing that I still need some time?"

Tony grabbed her body back to his. He loved the way her breasts melted into his chest. "I understand," he gave to her, kissing her soft pink lips once more. "You'll be leaving here next month, and I'll be right by your side," he softly expressed, giving her a peck on her forehead and looking deep into her eyes. "You make me very happy, Amber and I'm going to do everything within my power to make sure you feel the same."

Amber closed her eyes and felt very special. Good Lord, Tony could very well be the man of her dreams!

# CHAPTER **TWENTY-THREE**

Tony Rivera was now the new man in her life. By default or by magic, Amber was feeling more energized than ever with a future to suddenly look forward to. She was making plans and setting up trips for them take, something she hadn't done or felt like doing in such a long time. He brought back hope into her life and she loved him more and more each day for that. She actually felt like she had discovered another soul mate. Time spent with Tony had been too easy and she felt like she had known him her whole life. He introduced a spiritual connection to her rather than a emotional one.

He was humorous too, something her ex never possessed and she was so thankful for the non-comparatives. Tony was **IT** for her. They were both Air Signs; him being an Aquarius, she a Libra. They were also an ideal match in that Amber was always so mesmerized at how smart he was. Her ex was an intellectual too (an Aries) but there was something different about Tony when they could talk for hours without sex ever being a factor and they became instantaneous best friends. There was a graciousness and mutual respect between them that was also exceptional. Tony saw in Amber a lady worthy of his affections, while Amber found a gentleman who gave her the freedom to be herself. Always the constant romantic, Amber was appeasing to Tony and loved her social skills and admired her natural beauty, light-heartedness and reliable silliness. She could envision the rest of her life with him and Amber was finally appreciating living at the moment, her sadness slowly vanishing, dissipated until it was gone.

Tony, in addition was also a very generous man; openhanded to charities, liberal with his investments and happy to spend, so when Tony was invited to attend an event, he usually went and this time he had a steady date.

Amber and Tony were seen all around town at several ceremonies making appearances as a couple and accepting various awards. So when Tony was asked to fly across the country on the spur of the moment, he usually dropped everything and attended. He had people he trusted to oversee his business affairs and it opened up opportunities to take Amber away on several impromptu vacations.

## Manhattan, New York

Amber hugged Tony near, trying to get warm from the Hudson River's frosty air.

They were on the Staten Island Ferry, taking a tour of the skyline and the Statue of Liberty. Amber had never been to New York and Tony didn't hesitate to show her all the tourist sites. Tony lived there once, only for a few years back in the 1980's when he was trying to get a project off the ground and knew his way around town. They visited the Empire State Building, Rockefeller Center, Radio City Music Hall, Ellis Island and American Museum of Natural History, Central Park and lastly, a Ground Zero Museum.

Amber was in awe of every little thing, not only because she had never seen New York City, but because

Tony was so knowledgeable about everything that Amber felt like she could listen to him talk for hours with no end in sight. His voice was low and sexy, smooth and almost lyrical; she was so mentally transfixed on him she wondered how she was ever able to carry on a chat with her pompous ex husband always trying to monopolize any conversation.

Back at the Crowne Plaza Hotel in Times Square, Tony and Amber were in bed keeping each other warm when Amber finally declared the words "I love you."

Tony simply smiled, "Really?"

Amber closed her eyes, "Yes, really, I love you."

Tony brought her body in closer to his. The heat from his naked chest paralyzed Amber in that she never wanted to leave the safety of his arms around her or feeling that close to another human being ever again.

Kissing the tip of her forehead resting languidly on his upper body, he relayed, "And not just because you flied out here first class?"

Amber started to giggle and strained her neck to kiss his lips, "No silly—well OK, maybe that did have something to do with it."

Tony didn't think it was funny and over-powered her and stretched out her arms and held them against her head. "I'm gonna make you pay for that remark."

Amber knew he was just kidding when she fathomed the lust still in his words, "I bet you will."

Right where he wanted her, Tony opened up her mouth with his tongue and kissed her long and deep, then released his leverage so that she could embrace him back in return while he cupped one breast to his mouth and suckled, licked until Amber panted with anticipation.

"God," he breathed between bussing her skin down towards on her midriff, "I can never get enough of you."

Amber reached up and caressed the center of his back first before laying her hands at the back of his head, "And I with you."

Tony positioned her lower torso to receive him and kissed Amber repeatedly, lovingly, passionately like there was no tomorrow and happily watched her as they visited their final highlight of the day. Pushing and holding her body near, he grabbed at the base of her buttocks and felt Amber quiver beneath him as she reached another orgasm. Two more thrusts for him and he let go all that was bothering him, all that was holding him back from fully caring about another woman and rejoiced in the euphoria of loving someone so deep.

Not moving in the slightest, he began nipping at her ear when Amber brought his body in closer, if that was possible and whispered at his neck "I love you" again.

And this time, she really meant it.

# CHAPTER **TWENTY-FOUR**

*California*

Tony handed the valet his Range Rover keys as he opened up Amber's passenger side door. "Park it in a nice secluded area if you can, there'll be a hundred dollars waiting for you at the end of the evening if she remains unscratched with the same mileage."

"Yes sir!" The young attendant exclaimed, rushing over to the driver's side and plopping himself into the car.

Amber beamed up at Tony as they joined in unison on their way into Spago Beverly Hills, for dinner. "You are such a giving man Tony."

"I know," he said as he gave her an affectionate peck on her cheek.

It had been almost two years. Two years to the day Amber swallowed all those depressant pills. Tony wanted to shower Amber in gold, wanted to give her more than she was willing to accept. It was such a keen frustration for Tony; he wasn't used to a woman who was constantly refusing his gifts. He offered to set her up in a condo somewhere off the beach, but Amber said no. She wanted to wait until they got married. Tony would have to rush the wedding, he soon realized, and the pair set the date for the summer. **That** summer, which were only a few months away.

They reach the hostess and reception desk. "Anthony Rivera, I have reservations for two," Tony pronounced in a stern, steady voice. He presented the lady with his best laid back grin.

The attractive redhead beamed back at him, "Yes sir, your table will be ready in a moment."

Amber and Tony waited alongside other patrons when Tony grabbed Amber and kissed her lightly on her lips. "God, you're beautiful."

"No, you are," she said, returning his thoughtfulness. Amber went to embrace him; she was feeling more than secure lately and welcomed his repeated affection.

"Hello Mr. Sanchez, your usual table?"

Amber's head whipped around and went white with shock. Her body rotated around within Tony's enfold as she stared at Mr. Sanchez flabbergasted.

Eduardo didn't expect to see her...**ever**. Remarkable that within the past twelve months he hadn't allowed himself to even think about her. Focusing on his ex-wife and the life they once shared brought forth-painful agonizing memories. After their divorce, Eduardo went through excruciating withdrawals. Not being able to look upon her face daily, handle her body, converse with her took him to depths of stagnation. He couldn't work, he barely even slept, the only device that kept him going was the simple fact that he knew she was at least still **walking**. That her latest attempt of suicide, failed, therefore, he knew her stubbornness could guide her through to rise above her depression. Stacey too, although in the beginning and hated to admit it, helped besides, with her words of comfort, her gentle caresses...her warm bed. He found himself going through the motions, trying to claw his way out of his former life, start anew, fresh, positive and back to his poise and self-assuredness. And now, all of a sudden, Amber popped out of nowhere and she was consuming him with her mere presence? **And, what the fuck was this?** Anthony Rivera—his former business partner with his hands all over Amber?

Amber's heart dropped at the simple exhibition of her ex-husband holding that blonds' hand. **Stacey Somers**, she assumed, they were divorced, it was OK, but she didn't expect to feel grief rapidly neighboring her heart. Those agonizing months of trying to get him out of her system were torturous to say the least. The solace he brought to her body when they embraced, his sensuous kisses alongside her neck. He haunted her existence...but so did Peyton. Amazing how someone you once loved so deeply could vanish from thought by not seeing them daily. Out of sight, out of mind, she guessed. Her ex-husband and her little boy part of a far away memory, barely visited because of the grief it still surfaced. Eduardo looked the same, **damn him**, undeniably fine-looking and dressed to perfection. His hair was a bit longer than she was used to, but it made him incredible sexy and awfully hard to glance away from.

"Hi," Eduardo gave to her, still penetrating her stare with his green eyes.

"Hi yourself," Amber gave back to him, feeling Tony tug at her body.

The intense chemistry was broken when the hostess stepped between the two couples and announced that their tables were now ready. "If you'd follow me Mr. Rivera, your table is just this way—I'll be right back for you Mr. Sanchez."

Tony jerked Amber away from her ex's stare. He was feeling a bit protective of Amber lately and didn't feel a bit shy of showing so. They followed the hostess and were seated at a table.

"I never expected we'd bump into him," Tony said angrily, "you want to leave?"

"No, I can handle it," Amber lied, feeling her throat close up.

The hostess sat Eduardo and Stacey at their prevalent dinner table. What Eduardo didn't realize though, as they both squatted down, was that his ex-wife and his former colleague had been seated just a few feet away!

"Who is that Eduardo? Don't tell me that's Amber," Stacey mocked in skepticism.

Stacey couldn't believe the nerve of that woman practically eating Eduardo with her eyes. Amber was really plain, with no spot of makeup on her face, she wasn't even pretty, but yet, Eduardo couldn't keep his eyes off her! Eduardo didn't seem the type to be attracted to her naturalness. She looked nothing short of an Indian with all that long dark black hair draping all over her shoulders. How dare she ruin her perfect day! Eduardo barely proposed to her not more than two hours ago and wanted to surprise her by taking her out to celebrate and she had to deal with this crap?

The foursome suddenly found themselves across from each other. It's awkward, it's uncomfortable—it's just not right. Amber tried to stare Tony's way, but it was no use, she still saw her ex in the corner of her eye.

Eduardo suddenly found himself looking Amber's way every chance he got. He couldn't get over how well she looked. The pink hue returned to her cheeks, her hair had all grown back and glistened in the chandelier lights. The bags under her eyes had finally vanished. He felt incredible regret running through his veins at that moment. **He** wasn't the man who helped her to become healthy again; it must have been Tony. Good God, where would they be if only he remained?

"Would you stop gazing over there, you look ridiculous with your head jerking around like that," Stacey haughtily voiced, irritated with Eduardo not giving her his undivided attention.

"I thought I recognized someone from court," he lied, popping a shrimp appetizer into his mouth.

"I can't believe you married her," Stacey quipped, "She's not even in your class."

Eduardo bore into Stacey's eyes. She insulted Amber? It had been the very first time he saw Stacey's resentful border and he didn't like it.

Amber hated how her head kept turning to try to see if Eduardo had been looking at her. She couldn't take the suspense any longer and decided to see if he were still the same magnet that he used to be and stood up, "I'm going to the ladies room—I'll be right back."

"I'll be here," Tony smiled up at her. Amber leaned over and kissed him lightly on the lips. She then walked passed her ex's table on her way toward the bathroom on purpose and doesn't look directly at him, but felt his instant lure and reaction.

Eduardo's eyes were glued to her exit and he had no other choice but to stand up as well. He doesn't give excuses or apologize to Stacey but simply walked away. He barely had to turn the corner to the location where the restrooms were when he was met with Amber's sudden animosity.

"Are you checking up on me?" Amber whispered through clenched teeth.

"Why, no...I didn't know you'd be here," he whispered back. "What are you doing here?" Eduardo asked, scanning her body up and down in amazement.

"It's a free country, you don't hold regime over all the fancy restaurants in town. I can still go wherever I want."

Good God, why did she ire him so quick? He watched in awe as she headed toward the ladies room.

He followed her then reached for the back of her shoulder.

"Don't touch me," she abruptly stated, swirling around to face him. Good Lord, why did she have to bump into him?

"Anthony Rivera...business meeting?"

Amber could tell by his expression that he was bothered. **Good.** "No, he's my boyfriend," she lied, not wanting him to know that they were engaged.

"Your boyfriend?"

"I'm allowed to have one now, we're divorced," she spat out, crossing her arms across her chest. "So I guess that's Stacey, always knew you had it in you to upgrade."

Eduardo grinned then circled his eyes around her face. He couldn't get over how healthy she looked, the fire had returned to her hazel eyes and memories of rolling in bed together flooded his thoughts. "Yes, that's Stacey."

"She's so...**short.** However do you kiss her? Does she need a stepping stool?"

Eduardo's heart began to pound; Amber brought forth a dormant smile to his face. Good God, she's back. He always admired her repartee. "Would you like to meet her?" He asked, testing her to a degree.

"Maybe," she surprised him. "Interested in investing in another project of his?"

"No," he said out flat.

Amber smiled inwardly, she had ruffled him successfully and was inflated knowing she did so. She stepped into him on purpose, diminishing the space between them. Boring into his eyes she asked, "Do you still find me disgusting?"

Any other woman who would have tried that little attempt at misbehavior would have received ridicule, but with Amber, Good God, his resistance unraveled and he was completely captivated. He revealed in a sprightly tone, "You surprised me." Eduardo then took a step backward and began to walk away.

Amber was left with her jaw on the floor. He got the best of her? No way, Good Lord, he was still a conceited bastard! "You could have continued to ravish this body if you had just hung in there," she yelled at his back side.

"Still merciless I see," Eduardo scoffed, "And, to a certain extent..." He turned around but kept on walking backwards, "You could have surmounted mine."

**Mount?** Amber snorted—**him and his big fuckin' words!** She watched him amble away and in turn rushed to the ladies room and ran into a stall. Her chest was moving up and down sporadically and she could barely breathe. She closed her eyes and felt the tears burst and spread around her face. She had never felt anything that passionate and exceedingly painful since the days of them not being together. It was equivalent to the obsession she used to feel when she was married to his brother and she had to restrain herself from not being able to touch him. **Goddamn that passion!** No one on Earth could rile her emotions the way that man did!

Amber arrived back at her table and found Eduardo sitting next to Tony? What the hell was going on?

Eduardo stood up upon seeing her then stared down at his former business partner. "Remember what I said."

Amber looked at Tony dumb-founded as Eduardo left and found her seat. "What the hell were you two just talking about?"

Tony started to laugh, "Funny guy your ex-husband; threatens my life with bodily harm if I ever hurt you."

Amber is livid, "How dare him!"

Tony stared at her angered expression. She seemed somewhat pleased. "Let's go Amber, I suddenly lost my appetite."

Amber grabbed her glass of water and started to sip when she noticed Eduardo and Stacey hand in hand crossing their table. Eduardo suddenly slowed down when he spotted Amber drinking.

"I see she hasn't stopped with the excessiveness," he let go disgusted. "Watch her with that, she can be a real pain in the ass."

Tony stood up and met Eduardo eye-to-eye. "You just insulted my fiancé Eduardo, so if you'd rather take this outside; I'm willing to meet you. Or should I embarrass the heroic attorney **here** while I kick his ass to the fucking floor?"

Several patrons look their way within hearing the sudden hubbub in the middle of the dining room. Eduardo decided to swallow his pride; after all, several of the regulars were his close friends. Good God, what did he just say? "Who am I to annoy Amber's **fiancée**?" He stated, eyeing Stacey then speaking directly to Amber, "When clearly he's rattled by the more suitable man."

Tony started to chuckle and tried to rise above Eduardo's cocksure attitude. "If you had just stayed...you could be holding what I have, and by our little conversation just a few minutes ago, I think you envy me."

"Envy you?" Eduardo jibed once again, "Why? So I could continue to put up with her stupidity?"

Amber came from behind Tony with the glass of water still in her hand and threw the liquid at Eduardo's face. "Taste that you fuckin fool!"

"What the—" Stacey screeched, bringing more attention to the scene. The water splattered clear across to her outfit as well, "Uh! This girl has **no** class!"

The water dripped all over Eduardo's face and partially all over his expensive suit, "That was uncalled for Amber."

"You conceited moron!" Amber shouted back at him waiving her arms in the air.

"Lower your voice," Eduardo sneered back at her. "Or at least let us all go outside."

Amber let go a heinous laugh, "While it's still none of your business Eduardo, we were here celebrating my sobriety—and you've just ruined it you bastard!" She tried to hush down and then came in closer to him and whispered into his ear. "Face to face with you Eduardo...seeing you again...all I want to do now is have a **fucking drink...**" Amber walked around them and out the entrance and ran toward the valet. "Find our fucking car!" She yelled at the youngster in shock.

Tony rushed to Amber's side and grabbed her body fierce. "I'm here for you honey...I'll always be here for you," Tony voiced, surrounding her body with all of his.

Amber grabbed his body back and embraced him in return. "Thank you Tony," she said continuing to fume. "I don't know what I'd do without you. I love you Tony, I **so** love you," she said, grabbing his face and kissing his lips.

Tony grabbed the back of her hair and kept her passionate stance contained with his.

They make-out in public for all the patrons to view. Amber then broke away from his mouth and laid her head on his shoulder continuing to enfold his comforting body when with reopening her eyes, she focused on Eduardo and Stacey exiting the restaurant behind them.

Eduardo turned his head away afflicted from seeing Amber kiss someone else. He was absolutely jealous from the range of passions she was able to stir and could bet a million dollars that her emotions were just as searing as his. He could almost envision the porno that Tony was about to undergo. Whenever he had an argument with Amber, the makeup sex was phenomenal. He wanted to slap her, he wanted to shake her, he wanted to **hold her**...but she was holding **someone else**.

# CHAPTER TWENTY-FIVE

Amber couldn't wait to tear Tony's jacket and shirt off. Passion so all consuming engulfed her and she hadn't felt that alive in years! She wanted to feel a man's hands on her body, languidly roaming her limbs, deliberately grazing her bare bottom and pawed at Tony's groin.

"I'm sorry about tonight—" Tony barely got out. Amber had practically attacked him and Tony could hardly keep up. He'd never seen Amber so incensed. She tore at his clothes as if she wanted to rape him. Who the hell was he to complain? He's wanted Amber naked since the moment they left her apartment! He's never wanted a woman more and as soon as he knew exactly what her intentions were he was a welcome participant. He began to undress her with rapid recourse. Amber assisted his hands and pulled off her clothes as well. If they weren't so engrossed with trying to pull at each other's garments, the scene would have been rather comical. Pictures were dislodged from the walls, chairs tipped over and vases were toppled and thrown to the floor. They reached the bed at last and Tony was a lunatic violating her body with his tongue and heated kisses.

Amber calmed down, the passion subsiding when she collected herself and enjoyed the soft moments of Tony's pleasure. They started to kiss again, his tongue inside her mouth, her passion returning in full force as Tony plunged inside her, thrusting again and again. Amber watched him as he brought his orgasm higher and this was where it hit her. Watching him...watching Tony's eyes light up...there was something different...their color...their tone...it was brown...not green...not green, but brown, not **green**...oh those eyes...his eyes! Who was this man sweating on top of her? This was not the man she used to love. She felt him reach his pinnacle, but she loses hers. She was thinking too much, concentrating too hard and remembered what used to be.

Tony lay still and motionless on top of her and felt her body relax and sedated. "I love you," he tells her, kissing her lips repeatedly.

Amber stared up at him then quickly replied, "I love you too, Tony," she let go, kissing him in return. "And I want to marry you, tomorrow...whadda say?"

Tony rolled away from her and cropped his head up with his elbow, "Tomorrow? Can't—gotta go to Denver in the afternoon, how about the following Monday?"

"We could fly to Vegas?"

"Yeah, look at the flights while I'm gone and book one to Vegas," he said, grabbing her chin and fingering her soft skin.

"So Monday, we get married, for sure?"

Tony picked up on her hesitation. "I would marry you tonight if I could, but let's be reasonable honey. What's the hurry, anyhow?" And then it hit him and he pulled his hand away from her face. "Was it Eduardo? Seeing him tonight? Is that why you're so heated up?"

Amber swallowed hard; she wasn't so confident at this point. Seeing her ex tonight was definitely tricky. She had been so sure of Tony lately and her emotions towards him and without warning, one meeting with her ex and she was doubtful? "I love you Tony, plain and simple," she let go convincingly enough; "I want to marry you."

Tony accepted her sweetness for what it was, "I want to marry you too, don't ever think that I don't. But honey, tonight was an eye-opener. Do you still have feelings for Eduardo?"

Amber sighed then lay back on the bed. Bringing her hand up to her forehead she confessed, "Honestly?"

"Please."

"It hurt to see him."

Tony believed her and then grabbed at her other hand and held it. "Why?"

"He brought back my son and all those painful memories of what used to be," she suddenly whimpered, feeling tears gushing down her cheeks.

Tony brought his body in closer to hers and wrapped a consoling arm around her upper body. "I'm here honey, I know, it took me a long time too, but with time and a whole lotta sex from me, you'll find yourself healed."

Amber started to laugh through her tears, "Anthony Rivera the cure-all."

"That's right," he stated, laying his head on her breasts. "I love you honey, it will heal, I promise."

Amber shut her eyes and with reopening them, relieved those few short seconds when she first saw Eduardo again, how she felt and how thrilling it was to see him once more and for the very last time.

She hoped to God she would never have to see him again.

# Chapter TWENTY-SIX

Trying to seize a deal on another project he had been working on, Tony whisked Amber away the moment he landed from Denver and back to New York. Vegas would have to wait for the time being, what was the big rush anyhow? When you truly loved each other, a piece of paper and a ring on your finger did not always equal commitment. As long as they were still together, in love and blissful there was always tomorrow.

The guest list for the venture was exclusive, upscale and nothing but rich benefactors. Investors as far away as Asia attended the black-tie affair.

The party was being hosted by one of Tony's oldest friends, Hubert Goldberg, one of the richest men in the world and he offered his generous Manhattan Penthouse suite for the event and Tony was nothing but grateful. He was assured that he would get the money he needed to fund the project in California; it was almost a done deal.

"Oh my God," Stacey said offensively.

"What?" Eduardo turned around.

**Shit, Pocahontas was there,** Stacey recognized. She looked different though. "She's here," she plainly said, pulling Eduardo away and around a corner.

"Who's here?" Eduardo wondered, looking around aimlessly.

"Your ex-wife," Stacey suddenly pronounced, watching Eduardo's facial expression turn cross.

Eduardo had been a major investor in several California ventures along the coast, so when he heard about another key commercial import/export building being excavated in Long Beach to help pave the way for a new structure and profitable business, Eduardo had no other choice but to attend the benefit along with the other financiers.

"Really?" Eduardo asked curious looking around him now.

"Why? You want to go back to her or something?"

Eduardo stared at Stacey jealous, she looked wonderful disturbed. "She was beneath me, remember?"

Stacey doesn't want to aggravate him, at least not until they were home alone. Eduardo mad was Eduardo sinfully carnal. Two weeks ago when they last ran into his ex-wife, Eduardo made love to her for several hours with no end in sight. Stacey was in sexual heaven.

"Are you going to go talk to her?"

"No; what time do you want to leave?"

"We just got here."

"An hour?"

"An hour—OK, just let me go and introduce myself to Judge Walker, he's sitting on a case I have in a couple of months back in L.A."

Stacey walked away from Eduardo and he was then left with a dilemma. Should he go back to the hotel? Should he go and talk to Amber? Should he just stay away? They have two different lives now and following two different plans. But why did they keep running into one another?

Amber was laughing with one of Tony's partners when in the corner of her eye she spotted him first. Doing a double take, her heart dropped at the sight of him standing there unaccompanied. Wearing an exquisite black Valentino tuxedo fashionably up to date, Eduardo looked incredibly gorgeous and stunned her senses. His posture reminded her of a commercial she saw just the other day where the male model was advertising a suit for a fine apparel company—posed and absolutely perfect.

Eduardo cautiously gazed around him while sipping his drink and caught Amber's stare. His body relaxed and his shoulders slumped at the mere sight of her.

No one else could have been in that room, their eyes lock and hold. Standing several feet away from one another, passersby dissolve on all sides.

Amber looked amazing. Her hair was done up in a French twist, with several different curls falling about her features. Diamond earrings dangled on opposite sides of her made-up face. She wore a long pink satin dress with matching shoes, her guise so remarkable, she looked as if she just stepped out of a bridal magazine.

Amber pretended not to see him and hurried out of an open French door that led out to the expansive balcony area. Eduardo followed her lead and dashed out simultaneously, both of them trying to steer clear of one another but neither one of them accomplishing the feat.

On top of the Manhattan penthouse suite where the party was being held the view outside was breath-taking. A spectacular panorama of Central Park, the penthouse was every bit amazing and what you'd picture as the ultimate in sophistication. A sister building to the St. Urban, the French design was a masterpiece with a high mansard roof, a domed corner tower and billowing curves. Built in 1906, the Goldberg's owned the Penthouse Suite on top of the St. Sebastian.

Amber didn't have to turn around; she knew he was there and she closed her eyes to step toward the edge and felt a little dizzy by the lethal combination of her ex's cologne and the devastating view from afar.

She stared straight ahead of her, "We have to stop bumping into each other like this."

Eduardo stood directly behind her. Amber's dress declined at the base of her waist and a tiny white diamond at the end of her necklace plummeted down the center of her back. He felt an impulse to touch it and caress the area that was exposed toward the front to her bosoms. Good God, the feeling was torture and he to shove his hands down his pant pockets from the temptation to do so. He came into Amber's peripheral view. "Trust me; I'm not doing this on purpose."

Amber heard the frivolity in his voice and smiled. Still looking straight out in front of her, she said, "Never thought I'd be seeing you in New York."

"Didn't know we had mutual business associates."

"They're not mine, they're Tony's, I'm just a decoration," she expressed, gazing down at all the amazing greenery, twinkling lights and skyscrapers beyond.

Eduardo swallowed his fun and continued to stare straight ahead at him, "So you're still with him?"

"…Are you still with her?"

Their bodies gravitate toward one another as they turn to look at each other fully now.

"Yes," he said, being brought in by her hypnotic gaze.

"I'm trying to move forward," Amber managed to relent feeling the magnitude of his gape.

"Me too," he said, looking away and across at the other buildings.

Love was a crazy game. Eduardo wanted to apprehend her, his sexual attraction to Amber besieged him. Amber desired to grab him to her breasts, feel his divine mouth on her skin. But they remained steady—all the while keeping their conservative distances.

"We're leaving in a couple of hours," Amber managed to assert cool, calm and collected.

"Don't bother; we're leaving in," he looked down at his watch, "Fifty minutes."

Amber snorted, "A countdown, huh? Stacey couldn't wait to get the hell outta here?"

"No, that was my suggestion."

Amber could feel the tears swell up in her eyes. She turned away from his hardened gaze. "Well this is just ridiculous," she heard herself giggle; "If we're going to keep bumping into each other then we'd better become friends."

"I'm marrying Stacey in two weeks."

And he just nonchalantly spat that out? Amber almost burst into tears. Married? Her body twisted to gawk into his eyes, "Wow, you wasted no time. She's not pregnant now is she?"

Eduardo laughed sickly at her comment, "Yah-no, no she isn't."

That meant he wanted to marry her! Good Lord, she needed a drink! "I guess we have that in common then," she confessed, waiving her diamond rock in front of his face, "I'm getting married as well, soon—maybe even tomorrow."

Eduardo was about to go mad. His heart swelled to a point where he was about to fall to his knees. He felt as if he were going to have a heart attack. "I thought as much," he relented, nodding his head toward the ground.

"Well, if you're sure we can't be friends, then you'd better run along then," she teased, flipping her fingers over his head, waving him away. "See ya around," Amber revealed, revolving toward the perimeter again.

"Yah...see ya," Eduardo uttered, leaving her alone on the balcony.

Amber gazed over at her glass of Perrier water. Good Lord, she could really use something stronger! The temptation was so great but she was going on two years sober and had been so happy, thrilled at times, but now all of a sudden, she was lost and miserable, drowning from the short sight of her charismatic ex-husband.

Should she jump off the balcony? She sure did feel like it. Would anyone care? She thought about it for a moment and held back her inducement while feeling her shoulder being touched. Amber turned around and smiled at a beaming Tony. He grabbed her into his arms and picked up her body to twirl her around.

They walk arm-and-arm back into the party. "I'm going to go talk with a potential investor, meet you in ten minutes by the buffet?"

Amber gave Tony a small peck on his lips, "I'll be there." She then watched her fiancée walk over to his colleague and felt something wasn't quite right. Amber didn't have to look around to know full well that her ex was somewhere in close proximity. She walked away...gingerly, strolling about, smiling at other guests passing her by when she found a familiar face, Tony's friend, Kristen Goldberg, the hostess for the event.

Kristen Goldberg, Hubert's second wife, was a flamboyant Southern Belle with violet eyes and golden hair. Harvested from Georgia, Kristen met Hubert at a prestigious horse race. Coming from old money, Kristen didn't have to marry at all, but fell in love with Hubert's sense of honor and undying respect for women in general.

"Save me," Amber asked Kristen, watching her friend's eyes light up in wonder.

"From what honey?" Kristen asked in her Southern drawl.

"From the man behind me," Amber asserted, watching Kristen's eyes gaze at the rear. "No—don't look, I know he's there, I can still feel his eyes."

But Kristen did it anyway. The only man she saw behind Amber and looking their way was... "Oh my, you mean that sinfully handsome gentleman pretending to talk to some woman while his eyes undress you?"

"Good Lord, it's not that obvious, is it?"

"Oh honey, welcome that seduction, but by all means, don't let Tony see you," Kristen purred while gazing back at Eduardo one last time. "God help us all, the man is just too wicked for words."

Amber rolled her eyes and pushed along with Kristen, passing her well-stocked bar. Amber hesitated, then stopped cold, eyeing all the alcohol displayed on top of the shell: Scotch, Rum, Tequila, Schnapps, Liqueur, Brandy, Bourbon, Champagne, Wine, Cognac, beer and Vodka...**SKYY Vodka.**

Kristen was suddenly pulled away from another guest and Amber was left alone—alone with her sobriety, alone with the constant urges, alone with the painful, dull ache and alone staring at all the enticing bottles.

"Don't do it," she heard him say behind her.

Amber felt her body turning around and eyed Eduardo with his hands down his suit pant pockets. "Don't do what?" She asked in a seductive timbre.

Shades of their past come flooding back in tidal waves; their blazing encounter in the copier room when they once worked together, before their affair and before their supposed devotion; those awkward heated moments whenever Eduardo was around her or vice versa, one of them was always tormented with their unsuitable obsession.

He stared at her for a few short seconds trying to wash away the memory of their past and gruffly said..."What you're tempted to do."

She aroused him. Good, she needed that little boost of confidence, because Stacey was suddenly springing up behind him. By the fire ignited in her eyes, Amber knew exactly what **she** was thinking. Stacey wanted to make sure Eduardo was still hers.

"Oh honey, aren't you going to introduce us?" Kristen said, suddenly appearing out of nowhere and beside Amber now.

Amber sighed with relief and entwined her arm within her friends and purposefully gazed into Kristen's eyes and blinked her thankfulness for the rescue. "Kristen Goldberg...Eduardo Sanchez."

"Charmed, I'm sure," Kristen said awarding him her hand.

Eduardo's ardent smile amplified. "In no doubt you are," he said kissing her offer.

Kristen threw her head back in good fun. "Oh my, is it hot in here or what?" She flirted with him, fanning her face with her diamond-rimmed hand.

Amber was amused by her game and not a bit troubled by her flirtation with her ex because Stacey suddenly flushed red with annoyance.

"Don't we have other acquaintances we still have to meet sweetheart before we leave?" Stacey gushed, pulling at Eduardo's arm. But Eduardo wouldn't budge.

Amber simply smiled at him then raised her eyebrow to incline her grin. Eduardo stared at Amber's lips as she bit down on them. He returned her playful pleasures by presenting her with an overzealous smirk.

Having witnessed the obvious fire between the two of them, Kristen almost expired at that moment. Did he just make love to her with his eyes? She pretended to faint and brought her palm up to her heart. "Oh honey, where were you when I was searching for a husband? I barely know you and I already want to see you naked."

Eduardo laughed along with her, "Perhaps another time," he expressed still aroused, feeling his body being pulled away anxiously by Stacey. "It appears I'm being summoned, nice to have met you Mrs. Goldberg."

Amber watched Eduardo and his ladylove melt away through the crowd of guests.

Kristen then yanked at Amber and pushed her into a nearby corner. "You gonna tell me who that female connoisseur was, or do I have to beat it out of you?"

Amber started to cackle; she hadn't had this much fun in years! She thought about Tony suddenly and how much he needed Kristen's financial support. "Would you agree to aid my fiancée in his project?"

"That's blackmail honey, from where I come from, we shoot grafters like you," Kristen spilled out, watching Amber's eyes grow wide from the intimidation. But she was already going to offer assistance to Tony; his project was a first-rate transaction.

"Are you really going shoot me?"

"Oh honey, relax, you've got yourself a deal, now tell me who that man was; were you lovers?"

"No," Amber suddenly looked down. "He was my husband."

Kristen noted Amber's heartbreaking look. "Husband? You mean you ravished that body daily?"

Amber started to hoot, "And sometimes even several times a day!" She added, joking along with her. But that had been the sad awful truth she had recalled.

"What a scoundrel, he didn't even introduce you to his lady friend."

"That's OK."

"He's still in love with you if you ask me."

"No he isn't," Amber incredulously let go.

"How can you be so sure?" Kristen asked, peeping around the corner.

"He's getting remarried."

Kristen watched Amber's face turn from cheerful to gloomy. "What about my friend Tony?"

"What about him?"

Kristen noted also Amber's shaky voice, "What are you going to tell him?"

"What do you mean?"

"What I mean honey, is that it's quite apparent that you're still in love with **that** man, and I'm no fool you see, knowing love as well as I do, Tony is head over heels in love with my friend Amber."

Amber gulped. She knew that. Now that Eduardo had truly moved on with his life she needed to do the same. "You're wrong Kristen, I do care for Tony and I agreed to marry him. He's been nothing but helpful and gracious and kind and nice to me."

"...But love honey...you did not once mention love."

Amber suddenly let the realization sink in. She turned the corner to watch Eduardo hand Stacey her coat and head toward the door hand-in-hand. **She still loved him**, she realized. Never mind about still harboring resentfulness. Never mind about what she thought and the reasons behind him leaving, never mind about him being with another woman and she being with another man and the feelings they felt towards them.

Amber closed her eyes instantly and envisioned Peyton in his father's eyes. That little frightened boy who needed her arms around him for comfort and she never gave it to him when he asked for it. Never showed him she was sorry...never showed him. Good Lord, whatever she did, whomever she's met, Eduardo is whom she would always love! Eduardo Sanchez would always be her one and only true love...

"Tony?"

"Yes honey?"

"Would you come here and sit down next to me?"

He dropped what he was doing and ambled over. "What's wrong, love?"

Amber thought about all the days that she enjoyed being his date for dinner and on vacations and business events. The times they made love in the early mornings and kissed and held each other till they feel asleep at night. All those comforting words and in each other's arms, and that made her start to cry. She began to weep because she would miss his friendship most of all. She was really going to miss Anthony Rivera. "You've been nothing short of wonderful," she suddenly blubbered, "You're such a generous loving caring human being, and you'll make a wonderful husband."

Tony stared at her for the longest time before saying, "But not yours."

Amber then began to bawl in her hands when Tony grabbed her body near to his and held her shoulders. "I won't let you leave, you can't. I don't care that you don't love me as much as I do you—oh God, I love you **so** much!"

Amber continued to cry, "I tried Tony, I really truly did. There shouldn't be any reason why I shouldn't be in love with you. You're such a decent man."

"Please don't do this," he continued to plead with her.

He seemed desperate in his beseeching but Amber continued to whimper even more so within realizing how much she still loved Eduardo. "Tony, I'm so sorry."

Tony closed his eyes and held her body near to his until he felt her body slip away.

Amber had to step away, her heart was about to burst. "I'm only going to hurt you more."

Tony tried to swallow through pain, "Let me be the judge of that."

Amber continued to allow her tears to fall. "I love him," she finally confessed. "I was never to meant to be with you...I still love him."

# CHAPTER **TWENTY-SEVEN**

That following Monday, Amber learned from Victor that Eduardo had been downtown mitigating a case for Yazmine and Amber headed to Los Angeles to try to find him.

His name was everywhere and on everyone's lips when she arrived when Amber also learned that Eduardo had been in one of the courtrooms on the fourth floor from reporters talking about the case.

Amber followed two other observers into the courtroom and found an empty seat amongst the spectators inside the large room.

Eduardo was in the middle of his summation when she noticed he stopped in mid-sentence to pause to catch his breath. Did he know that she was there? Was their bond still intact? She watched him from afar as Eduardo spread his wizardry across the enthralled forum. He was still magnificent; his words, his eloquence, his demeanor, his rationale wherefore the jury should acquit.

Before she knew it, the jury was being dismissed and the court was being adjourned. Amber wanted to talk to Eduardo as soon as he left but noticed that he and a few others had walked across to the judge's chambers. Amber then noticed the blond at the seat next to the defendant, Yazmine. Her platinum tresses pinned tightly into a power-ponytail. **Stacey**, she realized and watched her from afar as Eduardo appeared back in the courtroom and walked toward the two of them. Eduardo awarded a smile to Yazmine first before setting his smile on his fiancé.

Amber decided that it was better to wait for him outside and waited patiently in the hallway, while piles of onlookers and media poured out of the courtroom alongside with her.

In between flashing cameras and microphones, Amber managed to get a good look at Eduardo while he stopped mid-point to give a couple of reporters a few lines. She couldn't hear what was said, but the verbiage took all of five minutes for the media to be satisfied. Eduardo then led his entourage of legal minds away from the circus and headed toward the parking garage where more reporters had been stationed awaiting anything else from the heroic attorney and his legal team.

Amber was still only a few feet away and not once had he turned around to notice her. Or had the feeling already vanish? Eduardo always seemed to notice when she was around, he admitted that once to her a long time ago. That he could always sense when she was in the room and vice versa.

Eduardo did hesitate for the moment, only to converse with one of his associates and took the podium again to give a speech about the day's events. Amber again, stood back with the crowd and watched, as everyone was silent, listening to his reply about his famous client and the vindication.

Amber nearly gave up when she noticed Eduardo leading Stacey and another attorney to their driver and limousine. Amber started to follow them, but held back until she knew it was a good time to approach them, but Stacey kept hovering over him as if he were giving her a piggy-back ride!

At that moment, Eduardo turned around but didn't see Amber surrounded by people walking in front of her.

Amber wanted to speak to him, but couldn't seem to find him alone. That blond had her hand wrapped between his now and hadn't cut him loose. What, was she worried he'd run away? Huh!

Eduardo still continued to feel odd and out of place, when Stacey looked up at him and wondered at his bizarre look. Stacey placed a hand on his cheek and kissed his lips lightly. Eduardo gathered her head and kissed her back. Unexpectedly, the third attorney, away from Eduardo for a second, summoned Stacey unexpectedly. Eduardo halted; gathered up some papers inside his briefcase and then paused to see the crowd lifting to expose Amber stationary before him.

For a split second he thought it was an allusion, but then realized it really was his ex-wife. "What are you doing here?" He asked with a mild smile embraced to his face.

"I-I don't know," Amber confessed, starting to walk backwards. She wanted to cry in his arms, she wanted to thump him, but didn't, couldn't, why? Was it Stacey? Was it the fear of rejection? Was it **that kiss**? Good Lord...it was **that kiss**! Eduardo was in love with Stacey now and he just declared his affection for her in public by that loving flaunt!

Eduardo followed her as she walked back to her car. She was wearing a baseball cap on her head with her ponytail pulled through its snap, that's why he wasn't able to recognize her before. But he knew, deep down inside he knew his ex-wife was somewhere in the courtroom.

"Don't follow me," Amber turned around halting him with her hand.

"Why'd you come here then? What's wrong now?"

Thoughts of Stacey and him kissing swarmed her brain again. The way he held the back of her head, the way she pressed her body into his—they were in love—it was way too late. "I just wanted to see you action. I wanted to tell you **something**—but you continue to break my heart." Amber subsequently turned around and ran this time; dashed faster than she ever could or thought possible. She barely reached her car when she felt her body being swung around and her shoulders being tightly clutched within his strong tight grip.

"Break your heart? We're divorced, you and I— we've moved on."

"Have we?"

Eduardo's mouth suddenly went very dry. "I can't do this anymore...this—these dramas—that you bring on suddenly, you're impossible."

Amber's tears halted. Oh how she loved this man! Her feelings were just dormant and clouded over by their son's death. They were still there, still **here**. She's been in love with this man since the day she spotted him walking across the lawn at her in-law's backyard. Why doesn't he realize it? Why does he believe that she's impossible? Their love was never impossible, in fact, it was simple...easy. "You said you would always want me," Amber declared, not caring if it looked hopeless.

"That hasn't changed; I will always care for you," he admitted gingerly, "But what took me months to realize and what I don't **want** is that mania in my life. That constant urge to be near you, inside you, no one should be that desperate Amber. I don't like feeling out of control...And you drove me out of it."

He was shaking her now. Amber was already nervous; there was no need to shake her! "So it's really over—my God—we really did it."

"Did what?"

"Find ourselves happy with other people."

Eduardo shut his eyes. No other woman could pull his heartstrings like Amber could. He suddenly found himself with an uncoiling stomach, "Yes...I'm happy."

Amber gazed at his uncertain facial expression, "How come I don't believe you? God, you're such an incredible liar! I could always tell when you're lying, and you're lying right now."

Eduardo stuck out his chest and released her shoulders. "I'm not being dishonest," he disclosed, "I'm truly happy where I am. I'm content, relaxed for once. I actually come home from a hard day's work and feel—"

"Happy?" Amber exclaimed, finishing his sentence for him.

Eduardo closed his mouth; her condensation was too much to bear. She threw his heart off balance. He stared down at her in that silly baseball cap. Visions of a small face echoed through his brain. Peyton...Peyton looked like his mommy.

"Show me how happy you are," Amber demanded, meeting his eyes staring through her disguise. "Tell me to go away, command to never want to see me again." Amber looked deep into his eyes...and there it was, passion, hot enough to burn and the lightness in his green eyes, verdant and ready to devour. After that Amber allowed herself to breathe and permitted herself to feel him; inside his expensive tailored suit, up and around his shirt, his muscular chest, encompassing his tie, wrapping her arms around his back and pulling his body near...closer to hers to mesh against her skin. And this is when she felt his arms embrace her in return. **Good Lord**, her heart was about to burst wide open; she never felt anything so soothing.

Amber shouldn't have done that...touch him as easily as she did and Eduardo shouldn't have allowed her to do so, but **Good God**, his body called out for the contact and raw passion and familiarity engulfed Eduardo and his instinct told him that he should be kissing her along with this pleasurable interaction when he leaned into her face and watched her incline to meet him, when—

"Uh-**hello**," Stacey stated in disbelief, "Am I interrupting something?"

Amber pivoted around and gazed at Stacey glaring at the two of them embracing. Amber let go of his grasp and withdrew, but Eduardo didn't allow her to venture off very far; his hand still remained on the small of her back, rubbing her ever so softly with his thumb.

"No—I, I was just congratulating him," Amber managed to conceal, extending out her hand and walking away from Eduardo's contact. "We've never formerly met, I'm Amber Sanchez...um, Eduardo's ex-wife."

Stacey shook Amber's hand, but quickly discharged it. "Nice to finally meet you Amber," she quipped, twirling her engagement ring around on her finger on purpose.

Amber took a quick glimpse at the rock and swallowed her contempt. She was then alarmed by how short she was compared to herself. What was she like five-foot four, maybe even five-five? Her beautiful made-up face was enhanced by a lovely shade of mauve lipstick. Looking every bit like Grace Kelly, her elegance, her humility shoved Amber into instant intimidation. Her cobalt eyes stared into her hazels and sent shivers up her spine, as if she was the favored cat who had just swallowed the canary.

Stacey lifted up her jaw and raised an eyebrow at her fiancée. Eduardo stood grave. Stacey couldn't believe the nerve of this girl. Showing up unannounced, dressed in street garb, faded jeans, athletic shoes, sweat jacket, looking every bit the schoolboy. "Where is your fiancée?" She asked on point.

"He's at home," Amber lied, noticing Eduardo's look of surprise in the corner of her eye.

"So you're still with him?" He asked point blank.

Amber turned to look at him; her heart ached to tell him the truth. Oh, she knew she should have, it was a tall tale she was about to unfold, but she was left with no other choice by that she-devil who suddenly terrified the hell out of her. Shades of high school resurfaced almost immediately; the popular cheerleader demoralizing the nerd. "Of course, I'm getting married in a couple of weeks."

Eduardo's incredulous look was icing on the cake. Amber won the gamble. Now if only she could walk away from the table with all the chips!

Stacey's heart dropped to the pit of her stomach. Her fiancée had a devastating look upon his stupefied face. Amber too, looked disheveled and uncertain. Stacey broke through their obvious chemistry boiling, and said, "How nice for you, we're getting married this Sunday, aren't we sweetheart?" She then stepped in toward Eduardo and draped both arms around his waist. Eduardo fundamentally wrapped his arm around her shoulder, but continued to stare at his ex-wife.

"Can we continue our conversation?" Amber asked her ex-husband noticing Stacey's unbelieving expression.

Stacey's mouth dropped open wide and gazed up at Eduardo wondering if he'd even contemplate on departing. Apparently he did, because Eduardo let go of Stacey contiguously and began to walk toward Amber. Again, Eduardo grazed the small of Amber's back with his hand.

"Eduardo?"

He gazed back at Stacey, "What?"

"I cannot believe you're leaving me here," Stacey whined, her hands on her hips.

"I'll be right back; I need a moment with my ex-wife," he explained, guiding Amber away by pushing her posterior when Stacey ran up to him and pulled at his jacket.

"Whatever she has to say, she can say it in front of me," Stacey demanded earnestly. "We have no secrets you and I, we've always been up front with one another and I would appreciate it if you'd be man enough to not go off with your ex-wife and discuss God-knows-what."

Amber swallowed hard. She didn't want to profess her love in front of Stacey anyway, what if Eduardo no longer felt the same? She would feel humiliated. "She's right."

"She is?" Eduardo asked incredulous.

Amber gritted her teeth, "Yes, I wouldn't like it either if my fiancée went tracing off with another woman!"

"This is absurd!" Eduardo suddenly professed, rolling his eyes. "Why do I suddenly feel like the rope between a tug of war?"

Amber's blood began to boil. Eduardo always knew how to anger her. "You conceited bastard! You're probably all puffed up please about this, aren't you? Well, I just wanted to know how you felt about marrying her, that's all, and now—I don't know **why**—but I suddenly don't gave a shit."

"I know it must be terribly hard to lose a child," Stacey quickly chimed in, trying to become the voice of reason, "But you two no longer need to be friends," she paused to shoot looks at both of them, "Whenever you're around one another, resentment always seems to surface. The farther you stay away from each other—the better for all involved."

Amber and Eduardo both shot looks her way.

"She's right," Eduardo let go, digging his hands down his pant pockets.

"She is?" Amber said, gritting her teeth again. "Well that's just swell," she exclaimed, throwing her arms up in the air. Amber turned the other way and headed toward her car only a few feet away. She did not expect her ex-husband to follow her, but he did, **damn him.**

"I'm not done."

"I am," Amber rapidly cut him off.

"You came here for a reason Amber, and for the life of me—I don't know **why**—but I'm so God darn curious, you're distracting me with what it is."

Amber's throat closed up. The fury in his eyes, the anger in his voice, his body posture, his erratic breathing, all pointed toward one thing—passion about to explode. Amber was the one. Amber was the only one responsible for such emotion. Was this a good thing? It was always a start.

Amber's eyes glided over to Stacey who suddenly approached from behind Eduardo.

"Excuse me, but I'm still here," Stacey forged in.

"And so you are," Amber sadly voiced, "We... him and I, have a turbulent history," she laughed at the realization, "And if you don't mind Stacey...I need to find some closure."

"Did you know that Eduardo and I were once high school sweethearts? So, like you, we have some history too."

Amber just looked at her and then closed her eyes. She felt as if she'd just been kicked in the gut.

High school **fricken'** sweethearts?!

Good Lord, Eduardo **did** lie to her about being attracted to Stacey from the very beginning! All her paranoia had been justified after all? She knew Eduardo upside down—right side up knowing full well he was always lying to her and his continued temptation; fibbed about being involved with her when he knew damn well he'd kissed her before, probably even had sex with her often, **oh hell**, she was truly aggravated now! Her eyes penetrated his shocked look.

"So the mania was merited after all?" Amber asked trying to justify her obsession. She stood aside from Eduardo and leaned over to take a peek at his high school sweetheart. "Have a happy life with Prince Charming," Amber quickly pointed out, "Make sure he never lies to **you.**"

Eduardo at once hovered over Amber and stood directly in front of her, blocking her view from his fiancé. He looked down into her eyes and pierced through the outer layers of her rage. Amber was livid, and when she was bruised, she would make very stupid, **impulsive** decisions. "Stop it," he said shaking her shoulders again, "Look at me." He then took down a deep swallow and waited until his ex-wife bore into his eyes. "I'm sorry," he told her delicately. He wanted to clarify the truth, but didn't want to injure her with it – his heart pounded a mile a minute. "Allow me to explain," he whispered to her so that Stacey could not hear what he was saying. "Meet me tomorrow morning."

"Where," Amber whispered back, continuing to stare into his darkened stimulated eyes.

"You know where."

# Chapter TWENTY-EIGHT

At two o'clock in the afternoon, the ambulance shut its siren off upon entering the horrific scene. Grabbing their medical duffel bags first, the two paramedics, or EMT's (Emergency Medical Technician) exited their vehicle to find a chaotic mess of steam and mangled steel.

Assessing the accident first, there were two automobiles: One skidded into an electric pole while the other shoved into a brick wall – two drivers...one dead on impact, the other hanging on to dear life.

"Looks like a head injury," the medic claimed, holding Amber's neck still so that they could put her head in a brace. Her scalp was also bleeding from a gash on her forehead. The medic quickly responded to her plight and placed a bandage around her forehead.

"Let's place her in the back," the other medic stated, strapping Amber's unresponsive body on the stretcher so that she could be transported via ambulance to a nearby hospital.

Amber was on her way to the cemetery in the rain. That was their supposed meeting location; the cemetery. When Eduardo mentioned 'where', Amber knew exactly where and she was on her way there to tell him how she felt when she was struck by something or some **thing**. She was on her way to the site where she thought she would be safe...the place where she thought could help them get together again, a place where solitude and reflection was always apparent.

Amber woke up in another hospital bed, but this time, her injuries were not self-inflicted. Upon her arrival she knew where she had been taken to and was totally coherent in that she was able to even ask a few questions along the way. She had been in a vehicle collision, they told her, a car accident and she had suffered a small contusion to her forehead and a mild concussion. She would have to be under observation at least another night or two, or until a doctor said it was OK for her to be released.

She had to get a hold of Eduardo...but how? He had changed all his numbers a few years back!


Meanwhile, Eduardo materialized at the cemetery alone; full of anticipation upon arrival, until it ended in the dark and five hours in a rainstorm. He finally gave up and gave in and felt stupid for being stood-up and even more foolish for hanging onto a dream that his former wife would want to reconcile their relationship. In general, his affair and obsession with Amber had all been a mistake, he quickly analyzed. Their liaison had come full circle and to its closing stages and everything that had kept them together had soon departed. He found it odd, in a way, how a love that commanding could be diluted so easily.

Eduardo departed the cemetery feeling a bit remorseful but concluded that he and Amber were better off being apart and going their separate ways than at each other's throats. Marrying Stacey was the right thing to do, he decided. He had a lot in common with her, she was extremely bright and he loved debating with someone who could actually speak with intelligence rather than with emotion. They never argued and if they did have a disagreement then it would be resolved by the end of the day. A once incessant demand of wanting to be with another human being had transformed into a quiet desire of tranquility and compatibility of the mind and not the heart. The fire and passion he once felt with Amber had now been redirected into an equal level of deep infatuation for someone new. Physical attraction had now altered into mental pleasure and Stacey **could** make him happy...she **had** made him happy in the past and his old yearning of wanting Stacey for his very own had been satisfied daily by being coupled with her. Stacey was easy, uncomplicated and a wonderful lover. She could be all things to him...if he allowed her to be. A learned love could be just as good for him as an obsessive one, and this would be the second time he would actually find himself **in love**.

Obsession was unhealthy, he determined, and for a man to be completely fixated on one person was also very dangerous. Their relationship was immoral; therefore, it would have never been successful. They would have ended up absolutely hating each other, he also determined. Hating each other to the point where just mentioning her name would have left a sour taste in his mouth and he rather not have that.

On his death bed, he finalized, he would like to reflect on his relationship with Amber as being bittersweet and a simple stepping-stone to his final destination, which would be to grow old with Stacey.

# CHAPTER TWENTY-NINE

Rain beaded down on the St. Thomas Church in Hollywood, California.  Outside the cathedral, it was grey and gloomy, but on the inside, it was cheerful and gay; a joyful day for all.

Eduardo Sanchez was about to get married for the third time and he was anxious about entering **this** union; impatient to finally close the door on his past and open another to a positive future.  No more drama.  No more turbulent passion.  No more enhanced conversation with a woman who drove him nuts.  He was an astute thinker, a peremptory intellectual, admired and accepted among his peers—why not sustain a personal relationship that could mutually benefit the two of them?

However he managed to stand on that altar was beyond his capacity to fathom at that point.  He felt a little queasy watching his future bride stroll up the narrow passageway toward meeting him.  Stacey looked radiant in her cream-colored wedding gown, her platinum tresses up in an elegant coiffure.

Eduardo next noticed Stacey's beam when she gazed up at him and met her eyes with bliss and that's when he realized he was doing the right thing.  After that, he grabbed her hand and led her up the steps toward the minister.

Eduardo's heart began to pound gradually while hearing the pronouncement that he still couldn't comprehend. The minister could have been reciting his ABCs – his mind off in another dimension...and then, without warning, his heart thumped out of his chest. The one statement he did hear clearly after "...if there was anyone here who thinks that these two should not be joined speaks now—" **was**...

"I have something to say."

The entire congregation turned to look at her. All who knew her—gasped at the sight of her simply standing there. Jackie started to beam and wail while other guests all around them began to look **her** way now while the intruder made her way in through the closed church doors.

Amber was in the center aisle, placed center stage and didn't look straight at Eduardo just yet. She did however, look all around her and at all the faces pinned on her and related, "I'm sorry, it will only take five minutes, I swear, then you can have your wedding, no one will have to return any gifts—I promise." She then locked eyes with Eduardo still up on the altar.

Eduardo was in disbelief, concerned and surprised. "I'll be right back," he just said, walking down the steps toward the center.

Tears swarmed her eyes instantly as Stacey watched her future husband hurriedly walking away from their wedding without her. **That bitch!**

Within seeing Eduardo strolling toward her, Amber walked backward and outside the church and underneath a curved wall away from the rain.

**What a familiar scene**, she then realized, only Amber had been in the doorway and Eduardo was in the rain. That was the day when Eduardo came by her house late at night to return one of Adrian's videotapes. It was the night she realized that her brother-in-law meant more to her than she could ever imagine.

They look at each other for the longest time, he in improbability, she, in heartache. He looked absolutely wonderful, Amber declared; his black tuxedo, crisp ashen shirt, a white boutonniere at his lapel.

Her nerves began to soften however, the moment she watched him dig his hands inside his pant pockets. She knew in her heart that Eduardo wanted to touch her...he wanted to contact her but he held back.

Having Amber stand directly in front of him brought forth emotions he determined just last night were dead. She wore a long pink coat, a knitted black and rosy cap; there was something white showing through the knitting, Good God, what the hell happened? He couldn't stop staring at her, she appeared tormented yet brave. "Pink" he said, trying to breathe.

"What?" She asked.

"You're wearing pink."

"I know, it's my favorite color."

"Mine too," he said, feeling melancholy.

Amber suddenly felt a rush of sentiment fall upon her. Good Lord, she didn't know how she was going to speak to him without blabbering! "I wanted to apologize for missing our meeting."

He stared at her and said nothing for a short second and then relayed, "You weren't there either?"

Amber gulped and her heart fell to the bottom of her stomach. He didn't show up? He wasn't there? Good Lord, rushing to the cemetery in the downpour and the car accident was unnecessary? He wasn't even there? What an absolute fool she was! What an absolute **idiot!**

Amber, at that moment, realized that Eduardo had truly moved on and he was actually pleased about marrying Stacey. There really was nothing else more to say. She felt like her whole world was about to crumble into an endless pit of woe. "No," Amber voiced, holding back the truth about the accident.

Eduardo gazed beyond her out at the rain falling for a moment and then stared at her a second time, "You interrupted my wedding...was there a reason?"

Amber glanced away at the cars rushing by on the street, splashing water onto the curb. "Yes, there was."

Eduardo stared at her uncertain. Why did she come here? What does she want now? Good God, why does she do this? Her endless ways of teeter-tottering his emotions that tug at his heart!

Amber began reaching for straws. "We're leaving California," she spat out without thinking, "We're going to start a new life in Oregon."

Eduardo's throat closed up. Good God, he wanted to tell her he waited for her now, wanted to hear her reasons for not showing up! "You're leaving then?"

"Yah," Amber continued to lie, feeling her heart about to jump out of her chest, "We bought some property near the coast and we're going to build our dream house, the one I always wanted."

"We?"

"Yes, after we're married—that's where Tony wants to live."

Eduardo closed his eyes then reopened them to glare out at the rain beyond. This was the reason why she was here; to say good-bye, to mend the fence, proceed on with her life too. "That's great Amber, I'm happy for you."

The emotions in his face were hard to read. Eduardo's usual irritated facial expressions were unreadable. "Are you?" She asked, her voice cracking by the minute. "Because the other day, I knew you were lying when you said you were happy. I mean, I **want** you to be happy, that's why I'm here," her voice cracked again with tears swelling up in her eyes; she bit down on her lip, trying so hard to make them subside. "To see if you truly were," she continued, "You're marrying her today...I guess...the answer is obvious."

Eduardo was at a loss for words. He didn't know what else to tell her. His heart swelled. "Is he...is Tony good to you?"

Amber finally contained her sniffles, "Yes," she laughed now, "He's a wonderful man. He's become a very successful investor now, which was why we bumped into each other in New York. We met at the Palm Desert Treatment Center when I was there," she stopped to catch her breath, "Tony treats me very well—he's a lot like you in a way...conceited."

Eduardo grinned, "I'm not vain."

"Yes you are," Amber smiled as well, trying not to look directly into his green eyes. Amber suddenly noticed that his expression dropped, "You've always known what you desired and knew exactly how to obtain it."

Their eyes lock and hold at that moment, so many memories dash inside her head. The first day she met him at The Sanchez household. In their backyard, arrogant as hell, walking around with his head held high; becoming friends, trying to fight her restraint, her feelings for him, meeting at family gatherings, fighting her feelings for him, working with him at Aldridge & Watson, fighting her feelings for him. The night they made love for the first time...fighting her feelings for him **now**; running around town spontaneously making love whenever they could, asking him to leave his first wife for her, recalling his refusal, slashing her wrist. Her coma, his rescue...her miraculous son! **Oh dear God**...the pain swarmed her heart instantly. Peyton swarmed her heart! "Oh gee," she cried gazing down at her watch. "I've kept you out here for almost twenty-five minutes!" She said, blinking back her tears. "Your bride is going to be furious!"

"Amber," he murmured, feeling his heart about to jump out of his skin.

Amber didn't hear him call out her name and walked away. She tried desperately not to fully cry. With every inch of willpower she had, she held back her tears and stepped away and back into the rain. "Good-bye Eduardo," she barely got out, allowing her tears to flow freely under the protection of the raindrops. "My plane leaves in two hours and with all this rain; I just hope I'm not delayed," she laughed, turning around and heading toward her taxi at last.

"Amber!" Eduardo finally got out.

Amber was about to get back into the car when she heard his shout. The urgency in his voice sent shivers up her spine. She thought for a moment he might have changed his mind.

"I'm glad you came here," Eduardo shouted back at her at last. "I'm glad to see you're healthy."

Rain dripped relentlessly on her face now, thank God, for Amber allowed the tears to fall as they may. The difficulty to express anything at that moment was choking her, but she managed to mouth out the words, "Me too," and waved farewell.

Eduardo stared at Amber getting into the taxi and then watched the vehicle as it started back up again and slowly drive off with her inside. Choking back his own emotion, Eduardo straightened out his tie and pulled down his tuxedo jacket first before he returned back into the church.

Inside the taxi, Amber turned her head around to watch his hasty exit back through the doors and felt her heart fall into her lap. Her hands were shaking and she couldn't understand why. That's when she started to panic and quickly turned toward the driver and stated, "Turn around."

As soon as the taxi drove back to the front of the church, Amber popped out of the vehicle and rushed back toward the entrance and flung the doors wide. She bit down on her lower lip as she witnessed Eduardo's backside walking down the aisle. Amber just stood there with riotous emotions buckling her to her knees.

**It was truly over**, she thought. Amber had truly lost and surrendered to the sight of Stacey, his new love, his modernistic wife—prevailing. Tears continued to run down her face, as she watched Eduardo reach his future spouse. Stacey looked luminous, her pearl dress draping off the sides of the platform, the gorgeous bouquets of white orchids only adding to her brilliance. She smiled down at him as he grabbed her hand from the lower step as he approached...

*Oh dear God in heaven*, Amber thought as she closed her tear-filled eyes to dart out the church. ***Oh dear God in heaven help me please, help me before I do something impulsive!***

# CHAPTER **THIRTY**

"Can you wait for me here?" Amber asked the taxi driver.

"Sure ma'am."

Amber slowly stepped out of the car then shut the door behind her. Standing immobile for a second, she first gazed out at all the endless grave sites.

Walking toward her son's grave, Amber recalled the day she buried her son. It was a horrible awful day. She thought she would never get over that day, and yet, here she was. The pain still there, only lessened like a dull, slow twinge.

Reaching the plaque at last, Amber stood directly over it and softly voiced, "Hi Peyton baby, mommy wanted you to have something."

Amber then sat on her knees and bent down to place a stethoscope on his headstone, adjusting it to where it looked like the plaque had been wearing it. Peyton liked to play doctor and she wanted him to have it. It was a real stethoscope, having purchased it through the Internet. "Now you can listen to the entire congregation of angel's and their hearts and make sure everyone in Heaven is in good health," Amber started to laugh, then quickly burst into tears. "I tried baby," she wailed, "I really did, but daddy loves Stacey now, he doesn't love mommy anymore—he's moved on and it's OK...mommy is just going to move to Oregon and buy a house there and find someone to love as well. I'll be back on your birthday though; I'll never miss your birthdays Peyton."

Amber then continued to cry until she felt her body come to release all that was holding her down. The guilt she harbored from being the one at fault and the love she once felt for Eduardo and after a few more minutes of resting by his headstone, Amber finally stood up to wipe her dried tears away, when she sees him...

A little boy—no older than Peyton—black hair shining bright even through the grey clouds and was running around the gravesites laughing and playing with something in his hand. Amber looked beyond at a couple who were kneeling at a nearby gravesite and assumed he was their son, and began to walk away when the child yelled, "Hello!"

Amber then turned around to find the little boy hiding behind a tree. He was playing hide-n-seek with her but she could still see him; his legs and feet sticking out behind the trunk of a tree. A smile surfaced on her face and she waved a friendly hello. The little boy waved back but she still couldn't see him very clearly.

Amber turned to walk back towards her taxi when the boy's yell caused her to turn her head again. "Come and find me!" she heard him shout and Amber immediately turned toward his voice as the boy rushed from tree to tree. Amber laughed at the sight of him and joy straight away surrounded her heart. She watched him as he ran from one area to another, circling Amber finally, until the boy vanished completely in back of a massive carved statute of the Virgin Mary. Amber continued to search for the little boy, when **she sees him...**

Eduardo?

He's frozen, still—a long black trench coat covering his black Armani tuxedo. Amber looked behind Eduardo as he approached her and fathomed the black limo waiting in the wings.

"I knew you'd be here," he said, walking over to the gravesite as well.

Amber wiped the remaining tears away from her eyes. "I wanted to say good-bye to him...to let him know I'd be coming only on his birthdays."

Eduardo heard her voice crack and he choked back his own tears. He then glanced down at the headstone. Peyton, his little boy, would be turning six if he were still alive. He next looked back up at Amber, she had tears in her eyes and they both stood a few feet apart from one another, in uncertainty and still divided.

"I'd better go," Amber suddenly said, "I'll never make it to the airport in time," she conveyed, looking over at the limo again and then for her own transportation, "I've delayed my taxi long enough."

"I sent him away," Eduardo said suspended, unmoving, his hands still down his coat pockets.

"What?" Amber asked, looking all around at the area where her taxi used to be. "What did you do that for?"

"I'll take you to the airport," Eduardo offered, still unreadable and stagnant.

"No—you can't," Amber simply relayed.

"Yes I can, I own the limousine."

"No, I mean, you really can't. Good Lord," Amber said, rolling her eyes, "You're still so conceited Eduardo," and laughed sickly at his harsh naturalness. "Think about your **wife** Eduardo, I don't think your new wife would like me riding along."

"I'm looking at my wife," he presented her, green eyes penetrating her stare.

Amber's heart dropped. "But you got married," she cried, her tears quickly returning, "I left you at the church— you went back in. I watched you—I went back into the church. **I watched you** walk over to her, **I watched you** grab her hand."

"To tell her I couldn't marry her."

"What?" Amber asked, blubbering beyond repair, her heart beating by the sheer relief.

Within realizing Amber's reaction, tears streamed down Eduardo's own face. "Amber," Eduardo quietly voiced, shaking his head, "How can I marry someone I never loved?"

Amber burst with alleviation and she buried her face within her hands. Eduardo couldn't stand not touching her any longer and stepped in toward her and grabbed the only woman he's ever loved into him. They embrace instantly and Amber continued to weep, only this time into his chest. "But," she uttered through sobs, "You asked her to marry you."

Eduardo ran his hands through her hair and caressed the back of her head. "I was lonely," he let go, kissing the tip of her forehead, "She's the one who loved **me** and I thought she could carry our marriage with her affection, enough for the two of us."

Amber continued to liberate her sorrow on his coat and held him tight, "Like me...like me with Victor."

"I know," Eduardo voiced, burying his head in her shoulder, continuing to cry along with her, "I was going to tell you that a couple of days ago."

Amber subsequently pulled apart from him and gazed into his eyes with her disbelieving expression. "You **did** show up."

Eduardo looked down at her and wiped the tears away from her cheeks. Circling his eyes around her face, he reached up towards her hair then slid down her knitted cap away from her head. "I waited for five hours," he expressed, moving his hand over the bandage across her forehead. "I would have waited an eternity," Eduardo held, kissing Amber softly on her lips. "But the rain came down in sheets."

"The rain was really bad; I could hardly see the road."

Eduardo continued to run his fingers across her bandage then abruptly grazed his lips across her injury. "Something detained you...you were on your way."

With tears streaming down her face, Amber cried, "I was in a traffic accident—another car came into my lane and I veered off the road to try to avoid him when I hit a pole instead. Seven stitches and a mild concussion confined me from seeing you until this morning."

Their eyes lock and hold. Clutching each other once again, they cried in each other's arms for the longest time, releasing sobs of anguish, releasing sobs of pain.

"I love you Amber, I've always loved you," Eduardo admitted, holding his wife securely confined.

His words of comfort swarmed her heart—and she clutched him tightly in return—his arms wrapped themselves around her entire body; a sanctuary jam-packed with endless love.

Their mouths weld without more ado, as their kisses filled with tranquility and light suddenly turn enthusiastic and aroused.

"I could make love to you now," he whispered into her ear.

Amber opened up her eyes and smiled; her head still resting on Eduardo's chest when she voiced, "Well, there's always the limousine—"

"Want to fly to Vegas?"

Amber chuckled, "What for?"

"A wedding, I'm already dressed."

Amber continued to laugh when suddenly **she sees him**. The little boy again—peeking his head around the tree in the distance. He made her smile another time as the child continued to play hide-and-seek behind the tall oaks.

Amber suddenly blinked back her tears and pulled apart from Eduardo's chest when she realized what the boy was actually holding . . .

Good Lord...the stethoscope!

# THE END

"Mommy doesn't need an operation," Peyton stated, holding the stethoscope to his mother's chest. "She's still bree-ving," he voiced, looking up at Mrs. Lopez, "She's not dead-ed."

Mrs. Lopez shook her head at the notion, "Peyton mehiò, your father will be home any second now, let's leave your mother alone, it looks as if she's waking up now..."

By slow degrees, Amber gradually opened up her eyes to find that she could not see anything lucid due to the fact that the sun's rays were beating heavily down and clouding her view. It was hot, she was burning and her lips were parched and dry, cracked as she licked them. What the heck happened? Where the heck was she? Amber felt sick, nauseated and on the verge of throwing up. She felt hung over and she's felt that way before after drinking too much Vodka.

It was excessive, she knew that, but she chose to self-medicate because it helped to ease the pain. It was easier to do than to go through therapy, quicker to do than to hop in a car and sit down for a few hours with a therapist. Call it laziness, call it being selfish but Amber always chose the wrong paths.

Amber tried to focus once again but everything was a creamy yellow, a dazzling white...**and black.** Things were yellow, white and black...and then slowly the colors of forest green of the palm trees she had planted a couple of years back came into focus—then the crystal blue of the pool's water came into clear sight?

She gazed down and scanned over her entire body, she had been lying down, lounging and had been wearing next to nothing; her favorite Aqua-blue bikini top, but different bottoms she thought she threw away months ago.

Then Amber began to panic when she began to concentrate on the emptied bottle of SKYY Vodka next to her and the champagne glass on the other end table. Subsequently, she realized that she was lying in the same lounge chair and in the same Goddamn spot when she had lost her little boy!

Oh my God!

Oh dear God!

**Not again**, she thought, **Oh dear God, not again!** She just wanted her sorrow to end...when was she ever going to be granted a day of healthiness? Dr. Hayward had mentioned to her that she would be having some recurring nightmares about this dreadful day; she just wished they would stop. She remembered back at the Palm Desert Treatment Center when she would wake up dripping in sweat and crying from the very same dream. **Bad dreams** she believed were all too real and it took her a very long time to rest without having them or relying on the aid of depression or sleeping pills.

**OK Amber, time to wake up...it's only a dream...only a dream**, she thought as she closed her eyes again and prayed herself awake when she realized that she already was within hearing distinctive voices around the pool. Her eyes popped open again and in the corner of her eye, Amber could see them...really, really **see them**...then began to hyperventilate when she could comprehend Mrs. Lopez...with a little boy?

Oh my God!

Oh dear God!

Peyton?!

Amber covered her mouth over with her hand and then her neck when she watched Mrs. Lopez gather up Peyton within her arms to shelter him from Amber's fit of terror.
**"Oh my God!"** Amber let out, loud and unexpectedly.
It wasn't a dream, it had all been real and Amber swung her legs over the lounge chair and grabbed her head and after that, her heart as she covered up her mouth with both her hands. She was going to throw up...and then she did—and began to let loose the malicious poison that was the root to all her horrific hallucinations.
Out came the pain, out came the sorrow, out came her selfish decisions and out came the end.
Still on all fours, Amber wiped off her brow first before she reached out for her son. To affirm that she still wasn't dreaming, Amber yelled out, "Peyton?"
And she shut her eyes again, hoping that she was really awake and commanded through sobs, "Peyton, baby? Is that really you?" She watched in horror as Mrs. Lopez continued to shelter him from her bizarre panic. Amber needed affirmation **now** and cried out, "Mommy

needs you, **please**, please come here baby...please come here."

Peyton stood idle for a few short moments and then ran to his mother instantly. With two wide open arms, Amber seized her little boy...alive, well, and a little sun-burned on the tips of his shoulders from his mommy forgetting to put sun-screen on his body, but otherwise — OK.

Good Lord, Peyton was still alive!

Amber at that time buried her face in the side of his neck and simultaneously released huge sobs of relief, clutching him fierce from seeing him again and began to cry—no bawl—from the realization of what brought her to that point.

It wasn't a bad dream, it was **before** the nightmare's had began and in front of Peyton diving into the pool to save the puppy before Patience had darted after the tennis ball.

Amber continued to cry when she looked up to see Dusty Denver, the pool man entering on the lawn from the back gate, he was carrying chemicals in one hand while the other waved a friendly hello.

Mrs. Lopez in turn took a quick look over at Amber still holding Peyton within her arms and determined he was safe and walked over to greet Dusty.

Amber still held onto Peyton and didn't let him go when she noticed Patience wet from head to paws with a squishy yellow ball inside his mouth wagging his tail.

Amber then began to cry a little bit harder...

It was a scenario; a theory, if you want to give it a name. If a person chooses **Plan A** then **Outcome A** will be their ending, but if they choose **Plan B**, then **Outcome B** will be their destiny.  Amber chose Plan B which consisted of all the wrong decisions.

Ever wished you could go back in time and do it all over again?  Have a do-over, erase all your poor decisions and make the right or corrected ones?  Have you ever asked yourself...why did I get involved with that guy?  Or why did I cheat on that test when I knew all the answers?  Or why did I move to that city or why did I spend so much money at the mall?  Why did I sleep with him/her?  Why did you stay out all night or why didn't I go to the dentist months ago?

Well, Amber prayed for it daily and although it wasn't really a miracle like one would assume; it did turn out to be a result if she had maintained her path of self-destruction.

Amber waited patiently in the living room with Peyton still in her arms when Eduardo finally came through the door.

And when she sees him, Amber instantly darts toward her husband and cried in his arms hysterically.

After several hours of trying to calm Amber down Eduardo confessed to Amber that he did know Stacey back in high school and they were once boyfriend and girlfriend, but he never slept with her. In truth, he did find her still attractive, but no one could ever hold a candle to his wife's beauty nor could he ever love another woman as much as he did Amber.

Eduardo told his wife that Stacey had been fired that morning from the firm finding evidence that she had been inflating contracts and embezzling money from their clientele, and Tony?  Anthony Rivera was once his business partner, but they soon departed when he lost a substantial amount of money from one of their ventures and they amicably parted ways, and Kristen Goldberg?  She was a former client of his, suing her ex-husband for withdrawing their joint bank account and seizing all her assets and flying off to Brazil.   Amber must have read about her and her case from his files or by the newspaper…and the dog?

Eduardo nodded his head in the path of a sleeping Golden Retriever puppy and Amber closed her eyes and held her little boy sleeping soundly within her confine. Peyton had his thumb in his mouth while Amber kissed him constantly.

Later, the three of them walked together into Peyton's bedroom even as Eduardo gently let go of his wife.   Amber kissed her son's head one last time and protectively leaned into Peyton before laying him down on his bed to rest.  He was only asleep; she had to keep reminding herself…only sleeping and not…***gone.***

Grabbing her husband's hand, she turned into him as Eduardo collectively gathered her body near and gave her a reassuring hug.  Amber then gazed down at their son sleeping soundly and unaware of the horror his mother had went through.   Tears then began to fall again as Amber, after that, knelt down at the foot of his bed, raised her head up to the ceiling and prayed to the Lord, thanking Him for giving her a new start and for showing her what could have been if she continued to be temperamental, impulsive and emotional…and the road back to Plan A.

"Thank you Lord for continuing to make me feel special by the man that I love and thank you Lord for giving me a second chance with my son and showing me the true crossroad to follow…Thank you Lord, thank you…"

# OTHER GREAT TITLES BY TRISH

Unsuitable Obsession – Part One
Dare To Love – The Hollinger Series
Magnet & Steele
So Much To Lose

Visit Trish daily on her Website at www.trishafuentes.com

LaVergne, TN USA
14 February 2010
173071LV00004B/25/P